P9-EMR-502

The Best Advent Ever

by
Paul McCusker

Augustine Institute
Greenwood Village, CO

Augustine Institute
6160 S. Syracuse Way, Suite 310
Greenwood Village, CO 80111
Tel: (866) 767-3155
www.augustineinstitute.org

Note: Different versions of some of these stories
have appeared in the *Signs of Grace* series.

Creative Director: Ben Dybas
Cover Design: Lisa Marie Patterson
Illustrations: Robert Dunn

© 2018 Paul McCusker
All rights reserved.

ISBN-978-1-7327208-2-4
Library of Congress Control Number 2018959510

Printed in the United States

Contents

Introduction

Nicholas and Samantha Perry are twins. Nicholas is usually called Nick and Samantha is called Sam. They are both eight years old. They have a ten-year-old sister named Lizzy. Lizzy is short for Elizabeth. They also have a twelve-year-old brother named Andrew. Their parents are named Jon and Belle.

Nick and Sam have a good friend named Brad Wilkes. Brad comes to their house to play. He sometimes leads Nick and Sam into trouble.

Early last summer the Perry family moved from Denver to a town called Hope Springs. Hope Springs is near the

Rocky Mountains in Colorado. It is a town that has a lot of fun things to do.

Nick and Sam like Hope Springs. They visited relatives there when they were growing up. Their parish is called St. Clare of Assisi Catholic Church. Nick and Sam attend the parish school next door. Father Cliff Montgomery is the new pastor at St. Clare's. He is young and full of energy. Sam says he is handsome. Nick says he is smart. Dad says he looks too young to be a pastor.

Deacon Chuck Crosby is older and helps Father Cliff a lot. Norm Sullivan is the handyman for the church and the adjoining school. He is friendly and has an unusual way of thinking about things.

Our stories tell about Nick's and Sam's life in Hope Springs. Maybe theirs is a lot like yours.

CHAPTER ONE

Saint Andrew's Day

"Did you do your homework?" Sister Lucy asked her third-grade class.

Nick and Sam sat a row of desks apart. They looked at one another.

"The reading about Saint Andrew," Sister Lucy said to remind the class.

Nick sat up in his chair. He had read all about Saint Andrew the night before. "Today is Saint Andrew's feast day!" Nick called out.

"That's right," said Sister Lucy. "But

you should have raised your hand first."

"Oh, yeah," Nick said.

"What can you tell me about Saint Andrew?" Sister Lucy asked the class.

Sam raised her hand.

Sister Lucy pointed to her.

"My older brother is named after Saint Andrew," she said.

Some of their classmates giggled.

"That's good to know," Sister Lucy said. "What else?"

Another hand shot up. Sam's friend named Kim said, "He was the first disciple of Jesus."

"That's right," Sister Lucy said. She pointed to another upraised hand.

Billy Burke said, "He was hung on a cross."

Sister Lucy nodded. "He was crucified like Jesus was," she said as she turned to the board. "But he died on a different kind of cross. Do you remember what kind?"

The class mumbled without answering.

Sister Lucy picked up a piece of chalk. She drew an "X" on the board. "It was shaped like this."

"And he was hung upside down," a girl named Valerie said.

"That was Saint Peter," Sister Lucy corrected her. She paced in front of the class. "What else do we know?"

Nick raised his hand.

"Nick?" she called to him.

"The feast of Saint Andrew means that the first day of Advent is on Sunday," Nick said.

Sister Lucy smiled. "Very good. And what does 'Advent' mean?" she asked.

"Chocolate!" Nick said.

The class laughed.

Nick felt his cheeks burn. "But it does," he said softly.

What was so funny? he thought. Advent was the season that led up to Christmas. That meant his family would put out a large Advent wreath. It was round and had four special candles.

His family would also bring out an Advent calendar built by his great grandfather. It was wooden and had painted windows that opened like small doors. Each door opened to a little box with a scene painted inside. Inside was also a small piece of chocolate. Nick loved chocolate.

"What else can you think of?" Sister Lucy asked.

A lot of hands shot up into the air.

Some of the students said that Advent meant putting up Christmas decorations and the Christmas tree.

Some said Advent meant Saint Nicholas and asking for presents.

Others said that Advent meant Christmas carols about Mary and Joseph and angels and shepherds.

Sister Lucy laughed. "Then I guess we should thank Saint Andrew for having his own day so that Advent would start," she said. Then she asked, "Do you remember what the word 'Advent' means?"

Nick had to think. The word "Advent" always made him think of the word "adventure" and that made him think it meant something big is going to happen.

Sam said, "It comes from the Latin word *adventus*. That means 'arrival' or 'approach.'"

"Very good, Sam," Sister Lucy said. "What 'arrival'?"

One of the students said, "Jesus was born."

Sister Lucy nodded. "And what else is going to happen?"

The class was stumped.

"Jesus is going to come again," Sister Lucy said. "Advent reminds us that he came, and he is coming again. We are called to faithfully watch and wait."

Sister Lucy began to hand out papers. Nick was afraid they were going to have a pop quiz. A few students groaned.

"It isn't a pop quiz," Sister Lucy said. "This is a sign-up sheet for our Christmas pageant. I expect everyone to help out with the roles or duties."

Nick looked at the list. It showed the names of Mary and Joseph, the angels, shepherds, and the Wise Men. There were also roles without names, like the guards and the innkeeper and his wife. The list also had duties for doing things backstage.

Sister Lucy said, "Take these forms home to your parents so they can approve what you want to do. Bring them back on Monday morning."

Nick looked over at his sister Sam. She was smiling. Nick knew she would sign up to play Mary. She always wanted to play Mary but was never chosen before.

Maybe this year, Nick thought.

Then he thought of chocolate again.

CHAPTER TWO

Christmas Boxes

Sam's father, Jon Perry, was bringing boxes in from the garage. The boxes had been used when they moved from Denver to Hope Springs last summer. This would be their first Advent and Christmas in their new house.

Sam thought, *Opening moving boxes is like opening Christmas presents.*

"We want this one," her mom said to her dad. The box had *Advent* written in big red letters on the side.

Mr. Perry nodded. He looked at her like

a schoolboy waiting for an assignment.

Mrs. Perry pointed to a second box with *Decorations* written on the side. "I don't need that one now. Put it nearby for Saint Nicholas's day," she said.

Saint Nicholas's feast day was when they put up the Christmas decorations.

"I'll find a spot," Mr. Perry said. He picked up the box he had just brought in and took it back out to the garage.

Nick sat at the kitchen table. He was leaning over the sign-up form for the Christmas pageant. "Do I have to sign up?" he asked.

"You have to do *something*," his mother said.

Sam had already filled out her form. She had signed up to be Mary.

"Be a guard," Sam said. "You could wear a Roman outfit and carry a spear. That would be fun."

Nick shrugged. "Most of the boys in our class will sign up for that."

Their older sister Lizzy walked in. "Be an angel. Then you would have to *act*."

Sam laughed.

Nick smirked at her.

"I heard they've put wires above the stage so some of the angels will really *fly*," Lizzy said.

"Really?" Nick was suddenly excited. "I'll do that," he said. He wrote on the form.

Mrs. Perry looked unsure. "That doesn't sound safe," she said.

Mr. Perry returned from the garage with another box.

"Not that one," Mrs. Perry said. "That has Easter decorations."

Mr. Perry looked at the box in his hands, groaned, then turned around and went back into the garage.

Sam giggled. Her father was popping in and out of the door like a cuckoo clock.

Lizzy sat at the table with her sketch pad. "I heard a rumor that they are going to bring in real animals," she said.

"Live animals?" Sam asked. "What kind?"

"Sheep and goats and a horse and maybe even a camel," Lizzy replied. She was drawing something on the page in front of her.

Nick laughed. "Where would they find a camel?"

Mr. Perry came in with a large rectangular box. The box had *Advent Calendar* written on the side. He gave Mrs. Perry a hopeful look.

Mrs. Perry smiled at him and nodded.

Mr. Perry looked relieved.

"Where is the box with the Advent candles?" Mrs. Perry asked.

Mr. Perry shrugged. "I'll find it." He went back into the garage.

"Do you think it will snow?" Nick asked his mother. He was looking out of the large sliding glass door behind the kitchen table.

Heavy gray clouds had come over the Rocky Mountains. They settled above the town of Hope Springs like a large sheet.

"Would you like it to snow?" Mrs. Perry asked. She placed a box on the kitchen table and opened the top. She pushed aside packing paper.

"I would!" Sam said brightly.

"*Here* they are," Mrs. Perry called out brightly. She held up a box of candles. Then she carefully lifted out a large Advent wreath and candleholder. It was a circle with four holders for the Advent candles. In between the slots were carefully carved figures of angels and shepherds and Mary and Joseph and the baby Jesus. It had been in the family for as long as Sam could remember.

"Jon!" she called out. "I have the Advent candles and wreath here!"

Sam rested her elbows on the table. She looked closely at the figures. One of the shepherds' staffs was missing. The crown on a Wise Man had broken off and been glued back on by her mom. The angels wore flowing gowns of blue and gold. Their white wings were spread out wide.

Lizzy moved next to her. She looked at the angels with a smile. The two girls giggled. They had been talking a lot about angels ever since Lizzy told Sam she had seen her guardian angel.

"Where should I put the Advent wreath?" Mrs. Perry asked. She picked

up the wreath and took it through the doorway into the family room.

Mr. Perry walked in with another box and sat it on the counter. "This one isn't marked," he said.

Lizzy pointed to the side. "Summer clothes," she said.

"What? Where?" Mr. Perry asked.

Lizzy pointed to a small drawing of a t-shirt and a large sun on the side of the box.

Mr. Perry looked, then groaned. He took the box back out to the garage.

Nick looked at the boxes and packing paper. "Where's the chocolate?" he asked.

"Do you think they'll really have animals in the Christmas pageant?" Sam asked.

"Or flying angels?" Nick asked.

Lizzy shrugged.

I hope I get to play Mary, Sam thought.

"I put the Advent wreath in the middle of the coffee table," Mrs. Perry said as she came in from the family room. "We'll light the first candle tomorrow."

There was a loud crash in the garage.

"There must be a better way to spend my Saturday!" Mr. Perry called out.

Chapter Three

The First Sunday of Advent

It was Sunday—the first day of Advent.

Sam was dressed for Mass. She wore a purple sweater and dark green skirt. She stood at the sliding glass door in the kitchen. She looked at the iron-gray sky.

She wished it would snow.

Thumps and bumps and muffled voices came from upstairs. Sam knew her father was trying to get Nick, Lizzy, and Andrew up for church.

"Get up or we'll be late," she heard her father say.

Every Sunday was the same battle.

Her mother walked in. "Good morning," she said.

"Good morning," Sam said.

Sam's father walked in a minute later. "You both look very nice this morning," he said and gestured at their outfits. Sam's mother was wearing a green dress with patterns of flowers.

"Thank you," Mrs. Perry said.

Her father went to the counter. He picked up the glass coffeepot. "Do I have time for coffee?" he asked.

Mrs. Perry looked at the clock hanging above the sink. So did Sam. Mass started in half-an-hour.

"That depends on whether you should fast for an hour before Mass begins or an hour before we receive Holy Communion," Mrs. Perry said.

Sam giggled. That was a debate her parents had been having for as long as she could remember.

Mr. Perry put down the glass pot. "I'll wait," he said and winked at Sam.

Nick slowly walked in. He looked tired. He wore faded black jeans. His gray pullover shirt was untucked. He was carrying one shoe in his hand and limping because of the other shoe on his foot. He dropped down into one of the chairs and fumbled with the shoe in his hand.

Lizzy came in next. She wore a long tan skirt and a dark brown sweater. She carried her sketch pad, as always.

Andrew was the last to appear. He looked at a large rectangular box leaning against the wall. "Is that the Advent calendar?" he asked.

Mr. Perry nodded.

Nick looked up from his shoes. "The Advent calendar?"

"You don't care about the calendar," Andrew teased. "You only want the chocolates."

Nick smiled.

"Nothing happens until after we light the first candle this afternoon," Mrs. Perry said.

"Are we ready to go?" Mr. Perry asked.

The family made their way to the minivan in the garage.

***

The Perrys lived only a five minutes' drive from St. Clare of Assisi Catholic Church. There were a lot of hellos and handshaking as they saw people they knew in the parking lot. Sam waved to her friend Kim as they went into the church.

The church was already full of people. Some sat quietly. Some knelt and prayed. No one spoke so that those praying before Mass could talk to God in the silence of their hearts. Father Cliff insisted on it.

Sam noticed the big Advent wreath. It sat high on a tall gold stand next to the ambo in the front.

One by one the Perrys genuflected in the aisle and sat down in a pew near the back. The kneelers came down, and they all knelt and said some prayers. Sam heard old Mrs. Franklin nearby whisper a Hail Mary as she prayed the Rosary.

Sam prayed they would have a good Advent together. She thought about all the new things they would do now that they were living in Hope Springs.

She sat back and looked around. The church had a lot of greenery and red ribbons adorning the pillars and lining the stonework around the stained glass windows.

Father Cliff Montgomery and Deacon Chuck Crosby stood at the back. The altar servers took their places for the procession. A bell jingled and everyone stood.

The organist began "O Come, O Come, Emmanuel."

The procession stopped next to the big Advent wreath when they reached the front of the church. One of the altar servers lifted the candle he carried to light one of the large purple candles. Sam watched with wide eyes as the candle light flickered and then grew to a bright flame.

Father Cliff later talked about Advent in his homily. He said that Advent was like waiting for something wonderful to happen.

"We are like prisoners waiting to be freed from jail," he said. "We are like servants waiting for the King to come home. We are like Mary and Joseph waiting for their baby to be born. We wait with them. We wait in hope."

Sam thought about the Christmas pageant. Would she get to play Mary this year?

"But it's not like we're playacting something in the past," Father Cliff said. He pointed to the tabernacle behind the altar. "Jesus is here with us now in the Eucharist."

Sam looked at the golden tabernacle. The gold was glowing.

"We are also waiting for Jesus to come *again*," Father Cliff said. "Imagine the doors of the church swinging open and Jesus himself walking in."

Sam saw heads suddenly turn to look at the door as if it might happen. A few people chuckled.

"That's what Advent is all about," Father Cliff said. "The past, the present, and the future. And we're waiting. But it isn't a sitting-around kind of waiting. It is an exciting kind of waiting. It is a sit-on-the-edge-of-our-seats kind of waiting. We *want* it to come so badly that it bothers us. That's why we pray. That's why we cleanse our souls by going to Confession. That's why we serve others. We want to be ready when Jesus comes!"

***

At the end of the Mass, Mrs. Hecht stood up. She was in charge of the music program at the school. She was a tall woman with short gray hair.

She said, "This year the Christmas pageant will be in the main school hall. We will put it on the stage. All of the classes will help. Students should have taken home a sign-up sheet."

Mrs. Hecht held up one of the sheets.

She continued, "There will be a few new things this year. Maureen Sullivan is allowing us to use some of the animals from her petting zoo."

Some of the children clapped their hands.

"Everyone will get a chance to help," Mrs. Hecht said.

When she finished, Father Cliff gave the dismissal. The final hymn started. Nick leaned over to Sam. He asked, "Did she say anything about flying angels?"

Sam shook her head. *He thinks about flying angels almost as much as he thinks about chocolate*, she thought.

CHAPTER FOUR

Candles and Calendars

The Perry family ate chicken and cheese enchiladas for their evening meal. Then they went to the family room to gather around the Advent wreath. The sun was down, night had come. Mr. Perry turned on a single light in the corner so the room would be dimly lit.

Mrs. Perry placed the three purple candles and the one rose-colored candle into the holders.

Mr. Perry led them in a prayer from a very old leather-back book.

"Almighty God, Heavenly King," he said. "We thank you for this first Sunday of Advent. Fill our hearts with hope and expectation as we look to the coming of your one and only Son. Give us that peace which the world cannot give. Set our hearts on obeying your commandments and thinking of others ahead of ourselves. Call us to your kingdom, where you live and reign with your Son and the Holy Spirit, one God, forever and ever."

"Amen," said the family.

Sam lit the long wooden match. It hissed and sizzled. She raised it to the candle wick. The flame took hold and jumped brightly. She blew out the match and set it down in a small metal tray next to the wreath.

Mrs. Perry said, "Light our darkness, O Lord, and by your great mercy defend us from all perils and dangers of the night."

Mr. Perry leaned onto the coffee table. "Now let's talk about what we're

doing for Advent," he said. "We have a lot of things to do at the church. But I want to know what you've decided to do that's special and will help someone else. Andrew?"

Andrew was standing, and he leaned forward against the sofa. "I signed up to help backstage for the Christmas pageant," he said.

Mr. Perry looked at his oldest daughter. "Lizzy?"

"I'm going to do a Jesse Tree and decorate it myself," Lizzy replied.

A Jesse Tree was named after the father of King David. It was a big drawing of a tree and the branches had the names of the ancestors of Jesus. It was a way to show how the people of ancient Israel played a part in the Birth of Jesus.

Mr. Perry nodded to his youngest son. "Nick?"

"I'm going to shovel the driveway if it ever snows," he said.

Finally he looked at Sam. "Sam?"

"I'm going to help Mom cook our Advent Sunday meals," Sam said. "And I'm going to make the meal all by myself on Gaudete Sunday."

"Those are all good," Mrs. Perry said.

Mr. Perry sat up straight. "Now, there are two new things for Advent we haven't done before."

The kids also sat up. Sam wondered what new things they would do.

Mr. Perry said, "This year we are going to join a group of carolers and sing at the retirement home."

"Sing to *old* people?" Nick asked.

Mrs. Perry put a hand on Nick's arm. "Many of those people are lonely. It will cheer them up."

"They make me nervous," Nick said. "They always hug me at church and smell like medicine."

"What's the second thing?" Andrew asked.

Mr. Perry gave a big smile. "This year we're going to cut down our own Christmas tree."

The kids didn't know how to react.

"You mean, go up into the woods and chop one down?" Sam asked. They had always bought their Christmas tree before.

Mr. Perry laughed. "Our family owns a lot of land on the mountain," he explained. "That's what we always did when I was growing up here. That's what we'll do this year."

The kids looked at one another. They'd never cut down a tree before.

Nick suddenly stood up. "Now the Advent calendar!" he said. He moved to the other side of the room. Mr. Perry had placed the family Advent calendar along the wall. It had been in the family for over a hundred years. Theodore Perry, their great-great-grandfather, had built it out of wood for his children. It was almost four feet tall and three feet wide. The front was painted to look like an old red brick building with lines of twenty-four windows. Each window had garlands around it and a hinge that opened like a door. A number was painted just above each window. At the bottom was a big wooden door. It was to be opened last.

The sight of the calendar gave Sam goose bumps. There was something magical about the calendar. It seemed to look different from different angles.

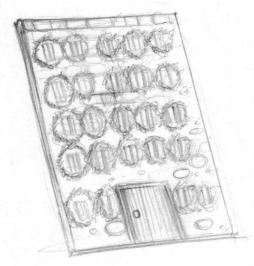

Sometimes the windows appeared larger and sometimes smaller. It depended on the angle. And the pictures inside the windows seemed bigger than they should be. It was what her father called an "optical illusion."

Nick reached for the first window on the top left of the building.

"*Wait*," Mrs. Perry said. "We have to talk about the rules."

"What rules?" Nick asked.

"The rules for who opens the window and who gets the chocolate," she replied.

Mr. Perry went over to Nick and put a hand on his shoulder. "In the past, we decided based on who had served someone else the best that day," he said.

Nick hung his head. "Oh yeah," he said.

"I'll open the door today," Mr. Perry said. "But we've added something." He looked to Mrs. Perry.

She smiled and said, "There's a piece of paper inside. It has a question about the story of the Birth of Jesus. The one who opens the door gets to answer the question first. Whoever answers correctly gets to eat the chocolate."

"What?" Nick asked. "That's not fair," he said.

"Why not?" Mr. Perry asked.

Nick stammered for a moment. He didn't know what to say.

"Let's give it a try," Mr. Perry said. He opened the first window.

Inside was a painting of a man kneeling next to an altar. Next to him was an angel glowing in white.

"This is the angel appearing to Zechariah," Mr. Perry said.

"The angel is telling him that his wife is pregnant with John the Baptist," Lizzy said.

Mr. Perry gave Lizzy a warm smile. "Good job, Lizzy," he said. He reached into the small compartment and pulled out a slip of paper. "Ready for the question?"

The family said yes.

"Since this is the first day, the first person who gets it right wins the chocolate," Mrs. Perry said.

Mr. Perry held up the slip of paper and read, "What did the angel tell Zechariah he couldn't do until his son was born?"

"Eat locusts!" Nick blurted out.

The family laughed.

"Wrong," his father said.

Sam raised her hand like she was in school.

"Sam?" her father said.

"The angel said he couldn't talk until John was born," she said.

"Right!" Mr. Perry said. He took a piece of chocolate from the Advent calendar and handed it to her.

"Aw!" Nick complained.

Lizzy held up a hand. "Wait," she called out. "Before Sam eats the chocolate, I have something to read to you."

The family looked at Lizzy.

"What is it?" Mrs. Perry asked.

Lizzy pulled out her sketch pad and opened it up. Sam could see handwriting scribbled on one of the pages.

"This is a poem I wrote this afternoon," she said. "It is called *'Twas The Night Before Advent.*"

Sam thought, *You never know what Lizzy will come up with next.*

"Stand up," Mrs. Perry said.

Lizzy stood up and held her sketch pad in front of her. She read out loud:

'Twas the night before Advent and
all through the house
No computers were stirring, not even
a mouse
The boxes were searched for the
family's big wreath
And the calendar buried in one far
beneath

*The children were wrestled to go to
their beds
Would Nick brush his teeth? Would
stories be read?
With Mom in her pj's and Dad
counting sheep
We all said our prayers and were
soon sound asleep*

*When out in the hall I could hear the
floor squeaking,
I went to the door and tried quietly
peeking
And what to my wondering eyes had
I found,
But my brother named Nick who was
sneaking around!*

*He was dressed in a robe that had
never been washed
And slippers all ragged and worn out
and squashed*

*His eyes—how they twinkled! His
    fingers were shaking!*
*He knew he'd been caught for the
    rule he was breaking,*

*"What are you doing?" I asked him
    real quick*
*For I knew it was too early to look for
    Saint Nick.*
*"Leave me alone" he said sharp and
    with dread*
*"It's none of your business, so go
    back to bed."*

*A blink of his eye and I soon
    understood*
*My littlest brother was up to no
    good*
*He said not a word, but turned with
    a jerk*
*Went straight to the kitchen and
    started his work.*

I stood 'round the corner and
     watched him act strange
I couldn't imagine what made him
     deranged
He looked on the counter, he looked
     in the cupboard,
He pulled out the drawers like Old
     Mother Hubbard

He looked in the spaces where things
     might be hidden
He even searched places he knew
     were forbidden
And then he collapsed on the floor
     with a groan
I sat down beside him and asked
     what was wrong

He spoke in a whisper with tears in
     his eyes
"Tomorrow is Advent," he said with
     deep sighs

*I really was puzzled about all of his
    hunting
"What makes you so crazy? What is
    it you're wanting?"*

*Nick looked at me like I had bricks in
    my head
I couldn't have guessed when he sat
    up and said,
"Tomorrow is Advent and surely
    Mom bought
The bags and the boxes of sweet
    chocolate."*

*He said while in bed he felt wild with
    a craving
To think of the choc'late he guessed
    she was saving
He finally knew he could stand it no
    more
And must find the place where she
    hid her great store.*

I knew how he felt, for I loved Advent
    treats
But knew what would happen if he
    sneaked any sweets.
"You have to be patient or there'll be
    a big fight.
"You'll wind up in trouble if you eat
    them tonight."

He knew I was right, though his
    stomach was growling
So he went up the stairs with a face
    that was scowling.
He stood at his door and then said
    really sad,
"Whatever you do… don't tell Mom,
    don't tell Dad!"

The family laughed and applauded. Except Nick. He frowned at her.

"That's not true!" he protested.

Lizzy looked at him. "*Really?*" she asked.

Nick shook his head and said quietly, "I *didn't* have tears in my eyes."

The family laughed harder. Finally, Nick allowed himself to smile.

Sam turned to her mother and asked, "So where *did* you hide the chocolate?"

Her mother smiled but didn't answer.

CHAPTER FIVE

To Be or Not to Be ... Mary

At school on Monday Sam walked into the main hall for morning prayer and the opening assembly. She sat next to her best friend Kim. Kim was born in China and lived in Hope Springs with her aunt and uncle.

"Hi," Sam said. She noticed Kim was holding the sign-up form in her lap. "What did you sign up to do?"

Kim smiled and said, "I signed up to be Mary."

Sam's face fell. "You want to be Mary?"

she asked.

"Yes," Kim said. "Why?"

Sam glanced away. "I was just wondering."

Kim looked at Sam's face. "You signed up for the same thing?" Kim asked.

Sam looked ahead. She didn't know what to say.

"But we both can't be Mary," Kim said.

The girls looked at each other. It was an awkward moment.

Father Cliff walked onto the stage to lead the students in morning prayer.

The entire time Sam prayed, *Dear God, what are we going to do?*

Later in class Sister Lucy walked up and down the rows of desks to collect the sign-up forms. She checked to see what the students had put down. She also made sure the parents had signed the forms.

She reached Sam and held out her hand.

Sam's hand was on the form, but she didn't offer it to Sister Lucy.

"What's wrong?" Sister Lucy asked. "Isn't that your form?"

"Yes, but I'm not sure now."

"Why aren't you?"

Sam looked over at Kim. Kim was looking at a book in front of her.

"I've changed my mind," Sam said.

Sister Lucy looked puzzled.

Suddenly Kim said, "No, you can't change your mind."

"What's going on? Is there a problem?" Sister Lucy asked.

"We both want to play Mary," Kim said.

Sister Lucy smiled. "A lot of the girls want to play Mary," she said. "You're not the only ones."

Sam looked up at Sister Lucy. "I should do something else."

Sister Lucy reached down and touched Sam's sign-up form. "Mrs. Hecht will decide. But she won't choose

you if she doesn't know you want to play the part."

Sam moved her hand off of the form. Sister Lucy picked it up.

"It's an important lesson in life," Sister Lucy said to the class as she walked on. "We have to learn how to compete, even when we compete with our friends. We also have to learn how to be good winners and good losers."

Sam looked over at Kim again. Kim still had her eyes fixed on her book.

Sam had a bad feeling about what would happen.

Nick sat next to Sam at lunch. He looked unhappy.

"What's wrong?" Sam asked.

"The angels aren't going to fly," Nick said.

Sam was confused. "What angels?"

"The angels in the pageant," Nick explained. "They're going to have painted cardboard angels flying on little wires. The angels on the ground will stand on a platform behind everyone else."

"So?" Sam asked.

Nick turned to face her. "*So* I signed up to be an angel because I thought I was going to fly. Now I'm going to stand on a platform wearing a choir robe and fake wings. I'm going to look stupid."

"Nobody will care," Sam said.

"*I* care," Nick said.

Sam shrugged. "Ask Mrs. Hecht to make you a guard."

"I already did," Nick said. "She said she has too many guards. She needs angels."

Sam sighed. "Yeah, well, it could be worse."

"How?" he asked.

"Kim and I are both trying to be Mary."

"At least you won't look stupid." He bit into his sandwich.

Sam knew Nick wasn't really listening to her. "I have to talk to Mrs. Hecht," Sam said.

"Good luck with that," Nick said.

Sam made up her mind what to do while she finished her sandwich. She would go to Mrs. Hecht and tell her she didn't want to play Mary.

***

Sam went to the school rehearsal room. It had a platform for a choir and a piano. Mrs. Hecht was sitting at her desk in the far corner. She was looking over the sign-up forms.

"Mrs. Hecht?" Sam said from the door.

"Hi, Sam. Come in," Mrs. Hecht said.

Sam stood in front of the desk. "May I talk to you about playing Mary?" Sam said.

"Oh yes. I saw that you signed up for her," Mrs. Hecht said.

Sam cleared her throat. She felt nervous. "I'm not sure I want to."

Mrs. Hecht looked at her. "Don't be shy about it," she said.

"I'm not shy, I—"

Mrs. Hecht interrupted her. "Take this." She handed Sam a sheet of paper. "Let me hear you say these lines."

Sam took the paper. "What?"

"Say the lines as if you are Mary," Mrs. Hecht said. She sat back in her chair.

Sam was baffled. She looked at the page.

"Just say the lines," Mrs. Hecht said. "Do your best. Speak clearly."

Sam stood up straight and read out loud, "My soul magnifies the Lord, and my spirit rejoices—"

Mrs. Hecht held up a hand and said, "You can do better than that, Sam. Mary is filled with joy. Sound joyful."

Sam started again and tried to think of how Mary felt at that moment. "My soul magnifies the Lord. My spirit rejoices in God my Savior because he has looked upon the lowliness of his handmaid. For, behold, from now on all generations will call me blessed."

"Very good, Sam," Mrs. Hecht said. "That will help me make my decision."

"But I—" Sam started to say. But Mrs. Hecht held out her hand for the page.

Sam gave it back to her.

"You're going to be late for class," Mrs. Hecht said.

Sam turned to leave. Kim stood at the door. She had a wounded look on her face.

"Kim," Sam said as she reached the door.

Kim moved away from her down the hall.

"Wait," Sam called out.

Kim spun around to her and said, "You sneaked in to talk to Mrs. Hecht about getting the part."

"Sneak! I didn't sneak! I went in to tell her that I don't want to play Mary," Sam said.

Kim eyed her. "And she had you read lines instead?"

"Yeah," Sam said. "That's what happened."

"Sure it did," Kim said. "Thanks, *friend.*" She stormed away.

"That's what happened!" Sam said again.

Kim kept going.

Sam put down her head and gave a deep sigh.

Now what am I going to do? she thought.

CHAPTER SIX

What to Do?

The next morning at school Sister Lucy called the class to attention. She said, "Everyone that signed up for a speaking role in the Christmas pageant will see Mrs. Hecht after lunch. She will want you to read for her."

There was a lot of whispering among the students.

"Except you, Sam," Sister Lucy added. "She said you already read for her."

All eyes went to Sam. She blushed. She felt like she had done something wrong. Kim shook her head.

"You can stay here and help me decorate the classroom," Sister Lucy said.

The morning slipped by. Sam thought Kim was ignoring her. She didn't like her friend being mad. But she also thought it was unfair. She hadn't done anything wrong. She probably wanted to play Mary for a long time before Kim ever thought of it.

Sam realized she was feeling resentful. *It must be wrong to want to play Mary and feel resentful at the same time*, she thought.

Later on, while the other kids went to see Mrs. Hecht, Sam stayed back with a few students to help Sister Lucy decorate.

Sister Lucy wanted Sam to hang up an old poster of a Jesse Tree. It was painted in beautiful colors of green and brown and yellow, like a real tree might look. On the branches were the

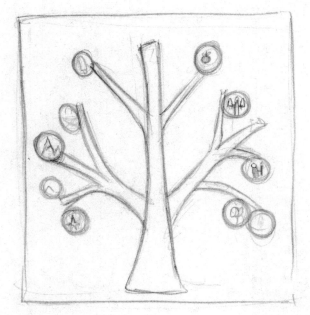

names of Jesus's ancestors written in beautiful cursive.

"Who made this?" Sam asked Sister Lucy.

"I did," Sister Lucy said as she pinned a corner to the large bulletin board.

"You're talented," Sam said.

"So are you," Sister Lucy said with a smile. "Mrs. Hecht told me you read Mary's lines really well."

Sam lowered her head. "But I don't think I can be Mary," she said.

"Because of Kim?" Sister Lucy asked.

Sam nodded.

Sister Lucy pushed the pin into the cork board and then knelt to face Sam. "Sam, I believe if God has given you a talent, then you must use it. If you are the best person to play Mary, then you should do it. Otherwise you're telling God that you don't value the gift he's given you."

Sam thought that made sense. But she also thought she should value her friendship with Kim.

Sister Lucy picked up a large drawing of the three Wise Men. She said, "If Kim's the kind of friend I think she is, she will be happy for you to get the part."

"She's not happy now," Sam said.

"She will be," Sister Lucy said. "Just like you'll be happy for Kim if she gets the role instead of you."

Sam hoped Sister Lucy was right.

It was two o'clock before Kim and the others came back from meeting with Mrs. Hecht.

Kim gazed at Sam.

"What happened?" Sam asked.

"I messed up reading one of the lines," Kim said. She looked like she might cry.

"Mrs. Hecht won't care about that," Sam said. "She'll be fair."

"It'll probably go to one of the older girls anyway," Kim said. "Let's forget about it."

"Okay," said Sam. "It's forgotten."

And she hoped it would be.

Giving the role to one of the older girls would be best. Then she and Kim could go back to being friends.

Or could they?

CHAPTER SEVEN

Choices

It was Friday, December 6, a feast day dedicated to Saint Nicholas.

A man who looked suspiciously like Deacon Chuck Crosby came to the morning assembly dressed as Saint Nicholas. He wore gold vestments with a dull red robe underneath. He had a long white beard. He carried a tall shepherd's crook.

Sam waited for him to say "ho, ho, ho" but he never did.

"My name is Nicholas," Deacon Chuck

said through his white beard. "That means 'victor of the people.' Many years after I died the Dutch called me 'Sinterklaas.' What does that sound like?"

Some of the students called out "Santa Claus!"

Deacon Chuck nodded. "That's right. The Dutch came to America in the 1600s and 'Sinterklaas' became 'Santa Claus.' Does anyone know where I was born?"

One of the older students raised her hand. Deacon Chuck pointed to her.

"You were born in Patara, Turkey, sometime around 270," she said.

"That's right!" said Deacon Chuck. "And I died as the Bishop of Myra around 345. Both are seaport towns in Turkey. Saint Paul had passed through them on his way to Rome years before I was born. But Turkey then wasn't anything like it is today. Back then it was part of the Roman Empire, and the people spoke Greek."

Deacon Chuck moved around the stage.

"What else do you know about me?" he asked.

Someone called out, "Your parents were rich."

Deacon Chuck pointed to that voice. "Very good!" he said. "My parents were wealthy, but they worked hard to help the sick in our town. Sadly, they both died because they became sick, too. So they left me all of their money. Do you know what I did with it?"

"You used it to help the poor and the sick," one of the older boys said. "You did it in secret."

"You're very smart," Deacon Chuck said. "Do you know how that has to do with Advent and Christmas?"

The older boy thought about it, then said, "That's why we give gifts at Christmas."

Deacon Chuck clapped his gloved hands together. "Very good! The tradition of giving gifts started because I gave gifts to help others."

He reached down and opened a large green sack. He pulled out fistfuls of small candy canes and began throwing them into the crowd of students. The kids shouted and laughed.

"These are candy canes," he said. "Tradition says that the candy cane is a symbol of my shepherd's crook— or 'crozier.' We'll hand them out to everyone as you leave the assembly."

And then he walked off of the stage. The students applauded.

Father Cliff came on stage and led them in a morning prayer that thanked Saint Nicholas for his kindness and faith.

After the prayer, Mrs. Hecht stood up and announced that she would let everyone know their roles in the Christmas pageant before the end of the day.

Sam had butterflies in her stomach.

***

Mrs. Hecht came in to Sister Lucy's class after lunch. The class went silent as soon as she appeared. She had a clipboard in her hand.

Sister Lucy waved to the kids.

"This is the moment some of you have been waiting for," Sister Lucy said. "Mrs. Hecht?"

Mrs. Hecht moved to the center of the class.

"Thank you for signing up," she said. "I believe this will be a wonderful Christmas program."

Sam wiggled in her chair. She saw Kim sit up straight and fold her hands in front of her.

Mrs. Hecht said, "Those of you in the choir have been working on Christmas music for a few weeks now. Now we need to concentrate on our actors. We have a lot of talent in this class. It was hard to choose who would play which role. But I've done my best to match the best person with each part."

Mrs. Hecht began calling out different roles and names. Some were for shepherds, some were for Roman guards, some were for townspeople, some were for the angels. She said Nick's name for one of the angels. Sam heard Nick groan. Then she called out the name of Brad Wilkes.

"What?" Brad said. "I signed up to

be a Roman guard!"

"I have too many Roman guards," said Mrs. Hecht. "Besides, I thought you would want to be with your friend Nick."

"Not if it means being a girl," Brad said.

"A girl?" Mrs. Hecht asked with a small laugh. "Angels aren't girls," she said.

"They *dress* like girls," Brad said.

Sister Lucy cleared her throat and said, "Brad and I will discuss angels and how they look *later*." She gave Brad a stern look.

Brad slumped in his chair. He sulked.

Sam looked over at Nick. He was smiling.

Mrs. Hecht went through the parts with spoken lines, like the innkeeper, the innkeeper's wife, Elizabeth, Zechariah, Joseph, and then ... Mary.

She looked at her list. "Mary will be played by Samantha Perry," she said.

Some of the girls gasped.

Sam's eyes went wide. Her jaw fell. She put a hand to her mouth. She let out a small squeak.

"*However,*" Mrs. Hecht quickly added, "I want Kim Lee to be the *understudy* for Mary."

Sam wasn't sure what that meant.

Kim's hand shot up. "Excuse me, Mrs. Hecht, but what is an understudy?"

"It means you will study under Sam for the role of Mary," she replied. "It will be your job to fill in if Sam can't do it for some reason."

Mrs. Hecht went on to announce understudies for some of the other roles.

Kim turned to Sam. Sam couldn't tell if Kim was happy or not. She turned back around and folded her hands in front of her.

"Rehearsals start on Monday," Mrs. Hecht said. "We have a lot of work to do in a very short time."

Sam was busy with school work that afternoon. She never got to talk to Kim. When the bell rang for the end of the day, Kim rushed off.

Sam watched Nick approach Brad.

"I don't want to talk about it," Brad said and walked away.

Nick said, "It's not my fault you were made an angel."

Mrs. Perry picked up all four kids in the carpool lane. Sam told her the news about playing Mary. Mrs. Perry was excited. Sam wanted to feel excited but couldn't stop thinking about Kim.

It's not fair, she thought. *I've been waiting a long time to play Mary. Now I am, but I can't enjoy it.*

***

That evening, the family gathered around a table in the living room. Mr. and Mrs. Perry brought out a box containing the family's nativity set. It was their tradition to set it up as a family. First Andrew put up the stable. Then Lizzy placed a cow and a calf in the back left corner. Nick put a sheep and a lamb in the back right corner. Sam carefully placed an old and a young shepherd just to the right of the stable. On the other side, Andrew placed a village girl carrying a basket. Lizzy placed a boy holding skins of water. Mr. Perry put the Three Wise Men on another table as if they were making the journey to the stable. Mrs. Perry put the crib in the middle, with Joseph on the right and Mary on the left.

Mrs. Perry then dug around in the box. "Where is the figurine of the baby Jesus?" she asked.

"You're not supposed to put him in the crib until Christmas," Lizzy said.

"I know that," said Mrs. Perry. "But he should be in the box. He isn't."

She emptied the paper out. Then she turned the box upside down. It was empty.

"Where could it be?" Mrs. Perry asked.

"Who packed the box?" Mr. Perry asked.

Shrugs from the kids.

Mrs. Perry slumped onto the carpet. "This nativity set has been in my family for years."

"We'll look for a replacement," Mr. Perry said.

"It won't be the same," said Mrs. Perry. "And it's an old set. We'll never find a replacement."

"How could the baby disappear?" Andrew asked.

"It must have been lost in the move from Denver," said Nick.

Mr. Perry put a hand on his wife's shoulder. "Maybe it was packed in another box. It'll show up."

"I hope so," Mrs. Perry said.

"Meanwhile, we can ask St. Anthony for help," Lizzy said.

"You lost the baby Jesus, and Sam and I lost our friends," Nick said. "This is turning into a *weird* Advent."

CHAPTER EIGHT

A Special Day for Mary

It was the Solemnity of the Immaculate Conception, and the Church was celebrating Mary's conception without Original Sin so that she could become the mother of Jesus. They celebrated this special day for Mary as a Holy Day of Obligation, a day everyone had to go to Mass. The students all got to go to Mass with their families on this special day even though it wasn't Sunday.

Sam saw Kim before Mass. "This is a special day for Mary," Sam said.

"I guess so," Kim said. "You know more about Mary than I do."

"Don't be like that," Sam said.

Kim tried to look innocent. "Be like what? I'm the *understudy*. That makes you the expert."

Sam could feel the anger rising inside of her. She didn't want to be angry, especially before Mass. "Why can't you be happy for me?" Sam asked.

"Would you be happy for me if I got to play Mary?" Kim asked.

"Yes," Sam said. She really believed she would be.

Kim frowned. "That's because you're Miss Perfect. Maybe that's why Mrs. Hecht chose you."

"I didn't say that!" Sam cried out.

Her mother stepped up to the two girls. "Is everything all right?" she asked.

"I have to find my aunt and uncle," Kim said. She brushed past Sam and went to find her aunt and uncle's pew.

Sam looked up at her mother. She felt like she wanted to cry.

Mrs. Perry brushed at Sam's hair with her fingers. "Give Kim time," she said softly. "She'll realize her friendship with you is more important than being mad about the role."

***

Every day the family had been opening the front of the windows on the Advent calendar. Inside were scenes about the Birth of Jesus and a slip of paper asking a question.

Some days Nick won the piece of chocolate. Other days he didn't.

Today the scene was about Mary meeting Elizabeth, the mother of John the Baptist. The question was, *What did Elizabeth feel when she saw Mary?*

Nick's hand went up before Mr. Perry had finished asking the question.

"You do that every day!" Andrew said. "Even when you don't know the answer."

"I know it today," Nick said.

"Well?" asked Mr. Perry. "What did Elizabeth feel when she saw Mary?"

"*Happy*," Nick said. He looked at the rest of them with a smug expression.

"Wrong," Mr. Perry said.

Lizzy raised her hand. Mr. Perry nodded to her.

"She felt the baby kick inside of her," Lizzy said.

"That's right. You may have the chocolate," Mr. Perry said.

Lizzy took the piece of chocolate.

Nick groaned. "But she was *happy* when the baby kicked," he said.

"Nice try," said Mr. Perry.

Sam and Lizzy helped their mother serve a chicken casserole dinner.

"Do you know what you want to make next week?" Mrs. Perry asked Sam.

Sam had been thinking about it. "I want

to make pizza with homemade dough."

"You want to make the dough your-self?" her mother asked.

Sam nodded. She thought it would be fun rolling the dough. She wanted to toss it in the air like the man did at the pizza parlor in town.

"That'll be fun," Mrs. Perry said.

The family ate the chicken casserole and then gathered in the family room to light the Advent candle. They prayed together. Lizzy lit the candle. Then she brought out a large roll of paper.

"Help me tape this up," she said to Sam.

Sam held one corner while Lizzy held the other. They taped it to an open section of the wall next to the Advent calendar.

"It's my Jesse Tree!" Lizzy announced.

The family gathered around to look.

Sam expected to see a drawing of a tree and the names of the ancestors of Jesus. Instead, Lizzy had drawn a large angel with a pair of spread wings.

"What is this?" Mr. Perry asked.

"I drew my angel as my Jesse Tree," Lizzy said.

The angel was tall. He had blonde hair and a shining face. He wore a white tunic with a golden breastplate and a golden belt. He had muscular arms that held a sword point-down in front of him.

"*Your* angel?" Andrew asked.

Lizzy nodded. Then she pointed to the feathers. "See? These are the angels that appeared in the Bible," she said. She pointed to the far left. "This is where the angels appeared in Genesis at the beginning of creation." She pointed to the far right. "And this is Revelation where the angels are helping at the end of the world. And everything in between is when they appeared to different people."

Sam saw a feather that noted the angels that stood outside the Garden of Eden. Angels appeared as men to

Abraham. There were angels at the top of Jacob's ladder. Another feather showed how an angel appeared to Moses. One angel was sent to punish King David and his kingdom. An angel brought food to Elijah. An angel helped a high priest named Joshua. The archangel Raphael appeared to Tobias. An angel saved the three young men from the fiery furnace. Another closed the mouths of the lions meant to eat Daniel.

Three feathers showed when an angel appeared to Joseph three times. A feather noted when the angels appeared to the shepherds. There was a feather to show how the angel comforted Jesus in the desert and another at the Garden of Gethsemane. Angels appeared to the women at the tomb. An angel freed Peter from prison.

There were also feathers dedicated to the archangel named Michael and the different times he appeared. Other feathers highlighted how the archangel Gabriel appeared to the prophet Daniel and then Zechariah and Mary.

Mr. Perry pulled Lizzy close for a hug. "You amaze me," he said.

"Why are you so crazy about angels?" Andrew asked Lizzy.

"Because they're important," Lizzy said.

Sam and Lizzy exchanged smiles. Sam knew that Lizzy had actually seen her guardian angel. Her parents knew it, too. Father Cliff also knew. But they hadn't told anyone else yet.

"We believe in guardian angels," Mr. Perry said. "We all have our own."

Sam wondered if their guardian angels sang for the shepherds when Jesus was born.

Nick took a long look at Lizzy's drawing. Then he pointed at the angel. "I wouldn't mind being an angel if I looked like *that*."

CHAPTER NINE

Rehearsal

This is a mess, Nick thought. He was standing next to Sam on the stage in the main hall at school. It was the first rehearsal on Monday afternoon.

A boy named Lance was on the other side of Sam. He was chosen to play Joseph in the Christmas pageant. Nick noticed that Lance kept staring at Sam.

"You're Mary," Lance said to her.

"I know," Sam said.

"I'm Joseph," said Lance.

"I know," said Sam.

"We're married," Lance said with a goofy smile.

Sam turned away from Lance and faced Nick.

"Help me," she whispered to Nick.

"But you *are* married," Nick said back to her.

"*You're not helping*," Sam whispered to him through gritted teeth.

Nick heard Lance giggle.

Mrs. Hecht began waving her arms. She was trying to get all the talking kids to listen.

Suddenly Sister Lucy clapped her hands three times. The sound was sharp. The kids went quiet.

"Thank you," Mrs. Hecht said. "I want all of the shepherds over *there*. And the Roman guards over *there*. And the angels over *there*."

Nick saw Brad try to sneak in with the Roman guards.

"You're an *angel*, Brad!" Mrs. Hecht shouted.

"Aw." Brad shoved his hands in his pockets. He walked over to Nick.

"It's not my fault," Nick said for the seventeenth time.

Mrs. Hecht called out, "I want Joseph and Mary in the center of the stage!"

Lance took Sam's arm to guide her to center stage.

Sam yanked her arm away. "Don't touch me," she said.

"But you're weak after a long journey," Lance said.

Kim came alongside Sam. "Maybe it's good that you got the part after all," she said.

Sam rolled her eyes. "Thanks," she said with a groan.

Nick and Brad shuffled toward the back of the stage with the rest of the angels. Nick looked up into the rafters. There were wires hanging down.

"I'll bet the cardboard angels will fly around on those," he said to Brad.

Brad snorted. "Give up, Nick. You are not going to fly."

There was a bang behind them. Nick turned to see his brother Andrew.

"What are you doing?" Nick asked.

Andrew was picking up a long board on the floor. "I'm part of the stage crew," he said. He carried the board and set it against the back wall.

"What's *that*?" Brad asked. "Is that a trampoline?"

Andrew looked. A small trampoline was leaning against a stack of chairs. He pulled it out and sat it down on its four legs.

"Does it work?" Brad asked.

"Looks like it," Andrew replied. Someone called Andrew's name. He moved off to another part of the stage.

Nick looked at the trampoline. Then he jumped onto the middle of it. He wobbled and then found his balance. He bounced up and down. And again. And again. He was getting higher.

"Hey look! I'm flying!" he said to Brad.

Mrs. Hecht's voice cut through the noises. "Nick! Stop messing around!" she said.

Nick bounced off of the trampoline and onto the stage again. He ran into

Brad. "Wow," he said.

Brad was laughing at him.

"It's better than standing around," Nick said.

Mrs. Hecht told the angels to line up. "I need to get you organized!" she said.

Nick looked back at the trampoline. He had an idea.

CHAPTER TEN

Festivities

Saint Clare's morning assembly became a festive time for Advent.

On December 12 they celebrated the Feast of Our Lady of Guadalupe by parading around the church. Then a Mariachi band performed hymns inside the main hall. The men in the band played guitars and wore traditional black and gold vests and pants with red sashes. They also had wide-brimmed Mexican sombreros. Sam thought the music was wonderful.

Deacon Chuck told them the amazing story about Our Lady and how she appeared to a young peasant named Juan Diego, who gave her message to the Archbishop of Mexico City.

Mrs. Perry brought breakfast burritos for the class that morning. She stood at a table in the back and handed them

out to the students. Sam noticed that her mother had tears in her eyes.

"What's wrong?" Sam asked.

"On days like this I miss my father," she said.

Sam's grandfather had played the guitar in a Mariachi band. He died of cancer before Sam was born.

Sam's grandmother lived in Arizona with her mom's brother and his family.

"You should call Grandma," Sam said.

"I will," Mrs. Perry said with a sniffle.

***

Saint Lucia's feast day was the next day. That morning the assembly was full of candlelight. The sixth-grade girls did a procession into the main hall. The girl in the very front wore a "crown" of candles.

Father Cliff explained that Saint

Lucia lived 1,800 years ago. She was killed because of a Roman law that made Christianity illegal. Many Christians were thrown to lions for entertainment. Lucia would not worship the pagan gods, so the local governor put her to death by a sword. Her feast day was often celebrated with candlelight because her name comes from the Latin word for "light."

***

Every afternoon the students rehearsed the Christmas pageant.

Sam got to dress in a blue and white peasant costume. Lance dressed as a peasant carpenter.

Lance kept staring at Sam during rehearsals. He often tried to hold her hand. One day he asked Sam, "Can we pretend to be married even when we're not rehearsing?"

Sam said a very firm "no."

Kim laughed for the first time in a long time. After that she acted like Sam's friend again. They helped each other learn the lines for Mary.

Lizzy showed her drawing of the angel Raphael to Mrs. Hecht. Lizzy asked if the angels in the play could look like her angel. Mrs. Hecht said yes, if Lizzy helped make the costumes.

Lizzy got very busy with two other girls from the fifth-grade class. They made gold vests that looked like gold armor. They made wings with wire and strips of white cloth. They used heavy cardboard to create swords.

Nick was happy. So was Brad. Even some of the boys who were playing Roman guards wanted to become angels.

One day Nick and Brad used the swords for a play-fight. They wrecked the swords. Mrs. Hecht took the swords away from all of the angels. "You will be *singing* angels from now on," she said.

The rest of the angels were not happy with Nick and Brad.

But they still got to wear the gold vests and the wings. Nick thought they looked like superheroes. He still wanted to fly.

CHAPTER ELEVEN

In Town

On Saturday the family went into town to shop for presents. It was a crisp day. It felt like it might snow. Sam hoped it would.

They all bundled up. Sam wore her favorite red scarf. It was soft and felt good rubbing against her chin.

Hope Springs was decorated for Christmas. Huge lights and garlands stretched across the main street from one lamppost to another. Big silver bells and candy canes hung from the

garlands. Metal wreaths adorned the cross bars on some of the posts.

"These are the exact same decorations they used when I was growing up here," Mr. Perry said to Sam. The family had split up to go into different stores. The trick was to buy gifts without the others knowing what you'd bought.

Sam walked with her dad. He was bright eyed and excited. He explained how Hope Springs had changed since he was a boy there. He talked about the natural hot springs that still served as a pool behind the Royal Hotel & Saloon. There was a legend that the famous cowboy Doc Holliday got in a shoot-out there after someone accused him of cheating at cards.

Her dad pointed out the old train station that was now filled with clothing shops. "Passenger trains don't come here anymore," he said. "Freight trains occasionally come through when the newer lines get jammed up."

They walked past a big building with five stories that used to be called Hayes Department Store but now had expensive condos in it. "I used to buy Christmas presents there for a dollar," Mr. Perry said. "I loved to ride up and down the old elevator. It didn't have buttons. It had a handle that you moved to get to the floor you wanted to go. For a long time, there was an old guy in a bright red coat named Hal who did nothing but run the elevator all day."

The Coliseum Cinema had a big white marquee. For years it was the only theater in town. Now they had a multiplex out at the mall. The Coliseum now showed movies for families and sometimes what Mr. Perry called "Art House" movies. During Christmas it was showing *It's a Wonderful Life* and *The Bells of Saint Mary's*.

Their dad remembered one big place

that used to be the Hardware and Feed Store. It had a big potbelly stove in the middle of the main floor. Old men in the town who wore suspenders and chewed tobacco sat next to the stove in rocking chairs. They told a lot of stories. There was also a table where they played checkers.

The hardware store was now a place called Hagan's Hand-Picked Books & Coffee. They stopped in for hot chocolate. It was the most impressive bookstore Sam had ever seen. There was an upstairs and a downstairs.

Sam found a book about angels for Lizzy. She also bought a book about the history of Hope Springs. It had a lot of pictures. She bought it for her dad. She had the cashier hide it in a bag so he wouldn't see it.

Toward the end of the main street they found Mrs. Perry, Lizzy, and Nick in front of a tall brick building.

Everyone was carrying packages.

"No peeking," Mrs. Perry said.

"Look!" Nick said to Sam and pointed to the building.

Sam gasped. She had seen the building a lot of times, but she never noticed how the front of it looked exactly like the building on their Advent calendar.

"This was the main bank building," her father said. "Alfred Virtue founded the bank years and years ago. Your great-great-grandfather Theodore Perry was best friends with Alfred. One year Theodore made a hundred of those

Advent calendars for the bank's richest customers."

"Are they still around?" Nick asked.

"There's one," Mr. Perry said. He pointed at the front of the bank. An Advent calendar just like theirs was in the large front window.

Sam looked up at a large sign above the door. It said in bold black letters, "The Virtue Curiosity Shoppe."

Sam went up to the window and looked at the Advent calendar. It was just like the one at home. Then she saw Andrew through the window. He was standing at the counter talking to an older woman.

"There's Andrew!" Sam said. She ran inside.

Andrew turned around when Sam rushed in.

"Hi, Andrew!" Sam said.

Andrew was beaming. "I *love* this place!" he said.

The woman behind him smiled. "I'm glad," she said. She was a slender-faced woman with round glasses and stylish brown hair.

"Hi, Cathy," Mr. Perry said. They shook hands.

"So, the whole Perry family came to visit!" the woman said.

Mrs. Perry gave her a hug.

Mr. Perry said to the kids, "You remember Catherine Drake. We went to school together. She is a descendent of Alfred Virtue, the man who founded this bank."

Sam remembered seeing Mrs. Drake when the family came to Hope Springs for summer visits.

"I'm so glad you moved back home," she said. She bent down and looked at Sam and Nick. "So, you're the twins," Mrs. Drake said.

"Both of us," said Nick with a wry smile.

"You've grown since the last time I

saw you," she said. She stood up and said to Mr. Perry, "I thought you'd come in to see me from time to time."

Mr. Perry hung his head. "We've been busy since moving back."

Sam saw a girl Andrew's age in the far corner of the shop. She had short black hair and big dark eyes. She seemed to sneak peeks at them and then retreated behind a display.

"Look at that," Andrew said. He pointed to a framed painting hanging behind the counter. In the painting stood two men. They wore old fashioned suits with vests and ties. The man on the left had a moustache and gold wire-framed glasses. The man on the right was clean-shaven and had bright blue eyes. Both men had a hand on a large globe of the world.

"The man on the left is Alfred Virtue," Mrs. Drake said. "The one on the right is Theodore Perry."

Sam looked at the painting and then at Andrew and back again. "Our great-great-grandfather looks like you, Andrew!" she said.

"I never really noticed it before," Mrs. Perry said as she took a closer look. "But he does."

"Even the hair," Mrs. Drake said. Then she waved to a glass case near the counter. "That's the globe of the world in the painting," she said.

The kids said "oooo" and went to look.

"Is this a museum?" Nick asked Mrs. Drake.

Mrs. Drake nodded. "I have a lot of my family things on display in here. I also collect a lot of items about the history of the town. But mostly I sell antiques."

"This is amazing," Andrew said.

Sam noticed the girl peeking out from behind a large wardrobe. The girl ducked away as soon as Sam looked at her.

"I don't think we're buying antiques

for Christmas this year," Mr. Perry said. "Let's go, guys."

Mrs. Drake said goodbye. But Sam noticed that Andrew made sure to be the last to leave. He kept turning around and around to look at all the things there. When Andrew reached the door, Mrs. Drake leaned down and said something to him. Andrew nodded. She said something else. Andrew nodded again, then he smiled at her and left.

When they were all outside, Sam asked Andrew, "What did Mrs. Drake say to you?"

Andrew looked back at the shop. "She said there's something really special she wants me to see in the basement," he said.

"What is it?" Sam asked.

"A special vault," Andrew said. Then he moved off. "I have more shopping to do," he called out and walked down the sidewalk.

Sam looked back at the shop. The girl she'd seen inside was at the window. She was watching Andrew walk away.

Sam wondered who the girl was.

Later in the afternoon Sam and Mrs. Perry went to the grocery store. Sam needed the ingredients for the pizza she planned to make for Gaudete Sunday the next day.

CHAPTER TWELVE

A Gaudete Adventure

Nick knew to stay out of the kitchen.

The family had gone to Mass first thing. It was Gaudete Sunday. Nick called it the "pink Sunday" because the candle was pink and Father Cliff wore pink vestments. But his mother kept telling him it was *rose*.

After Mass they found out that Uncle Clark was coming over for lunch. This made Sam panic because she was making her special lunch. Nick wasn't sure why it was a big deal to Sam. She was only making pizza after all. Mrs. Perry told Nick to keep quiet and stay out of the way.

"Keep an eye out and let us know when your uncle gets here," Nick's dad said.

So, Nick was standing by the front window and staying out of the kitchen. He heard a loud crash from a falling pan. Then he heard Sam cry out. Then his mother said something in soothing tones.

Nick turned to his dad. His dad was sitting in a nearby chair reading a newspaper.

The two of them shrugged.

Nick looked outside. The sky was still gray. But there was no snow.

A car drove down the street. It wasn't Uncle Clark. Uncle Clark drove a sporty black car.

Nick liked Uncle Clark. He was his dad's older brother and was an important man in the town. He was the mayor a few years ago. Now he worked to build up businesses and make the town a success. Nick suspected he was rich. Right now, he was building a big hotel and resort in the mountains. He believed people would come there to ski and to use the hot springs there.

Uncle Clark lived in the big house that had been in the family for years. He lived there alone.

"Why isn't Uncle Clark married?" Nick asked his dad.

Mr. Perry looked up from the newspaper. "He doesn't think he's called to it."

"Called?" Nick asked. "I thought you fell in love and got married."

Mr. Perry smiled. "As Catholics we believe that marriage is a *vocation*. People are called to marriage like men are called to become priests."

"Uncle Clark is like a priest?" Nick asked.

His dad laughed. "He wouldn't say so."

Nick wasn't sure why that was funny.

"He thought he was called to be a priest," his dad said. "He even studied to become one for a while. But then he realized God wanted him to do other things. Being married isn't one of them."

"Why does he live in the big family house alone?" Nick asked.

"He doesn't want to. He thinks we should live in it. But we were in Denver because of my work. He wanted to sell the house. I begged him to wait."

"We're back now," Nick said.

His dad nodded. "Your uncle intends to move to a new house after the resort is built."

"Will we move into the family house?" Nick asked.

Mr. Perry looked down at the newspaper. "Maybe," he said.

Andrew came down the stairs. There was another crash in the kitchen. He turned around and went back up the stairs again.

A gray pickup truck with big wheels and four doors came around the corner and pulled into the driveway. It was Uncle Clark.

"He's here," Nick said. "But he's in a pickup truck."

His dad put down the newspaper and stood up. "Uncle Clark is here," he shouted to the kitchen.

Things were suddenly quiet there. Nick thought he smelled something burning.

"Okay," Mrs. Perry said in a quiet voice.

Nick opened the door for Uncle Clark. He gave Nick a strong hug and then shook his brother's hand. "Everybody okay?" he asked.

"I think so," Mr. Perry said, with a nod to the kitchen.

Uncle Clark looked like Nick's father, but was taller, more muscular, and had a rounder face. He also had a shaved head. Today he was wearing a plaid

coat, jeans, and brown hiking boots.

"Hi, Clark," Nick's mom said. She was wiping her hands on a small towel. She gave Uncle Clark a quick hug hello.

"What's that great aroma?" he asked.

"Burnt pizza," Mrs. Perry whispered. "Sam is upset."

"Tell her not to fuss," Uncle Clark said. "We can go out to eat."

"It's all taken care of," Mrs. Perry said. "Let's go into the family room and light the Advent candle."

Andrew and Lizzy came down from their rooms. Sam joined them around the Advent wreath. She looked like she had been crying. No one said anything about lunch.

Uncle Clark led the prayer from the book. Sam lit the pink candle—

"*Rose-colored,*" Mrs. Perry said to Nick.

—and then opened the window on the Advent calendar.

"I'm glad you put that up," Uncle Clark said to his brother. "I still have mine, but it's in the attic somewhere. I haven't had time to decorate for Christmas."

"We'll do it for you," Andrew suddenly said.

Everyone turned to him.

"I love exploring in that house," Andrew added. Nick thought he blushed a little.

"You're welcome to come over any time," Uncle Clark said.

The scene in the Advent calendar was about Mary and Joseph going to Bethlehem. The question was, *Why did Mary and Joseph have to go to Bethlehem?*

"To meet with the censors!" Nick shouted out.

The family laughed.

"Because of the *census*," Andrew said. "Everybody had to go back to their home towns. Or something like that."

"Aw," Nick said. "I was close."

"You can have the chocolate anyway," Andrew said.

The doorbell rang.

"Who could that be?" Mr. Perry asked.

"The pizza," Mrs. Perry said and got up to answer the door.

Nick looked at Sam.

"Don't say *a word*," Sam said to him.

***

After lunch, Uncle Clark stood up and said, "We should go."

"We?" Nick asked.

"To get your Christmas tree!" Uncle Clark said.

The kids looked at each other with wide eyes.

"You mean, go out and cut it down?" Nick asked. He'd forgotten they were planning to do that this year.

Nick's dad stood up. "Whoever wants to go should get ready."

Mrs. Perry said she would stay home. "I have costumes to make for the pageants. Lizzy is going to help me."

Lizzy nodded.

"I don't want to go," Sam said in a sad voice. "I have to go scrape the pans I burned."

"We'll do that later," Mrs. Perry said.

"I want to stay home," Sam said firmly.

Mrs. Perry gently rubbed her shoulder. "Okay," she said.

"Then I guess it's boys only," Uncle Clark said. "Dress for the mountains!"

Nick and Andrew put on sweaters and hiking boots and heavy coats. They climbed into the back seat of the pick-up truck. Their dad and uncle climbed into the front. They drove out of the neighborhood and through town. A lot of people were out and about to shop.

Uncle Clark took the road up into the mountains. They wound through woods filled with pine trees and hills made of large boulders.

They came to a side road and drove up to a fence. It was the site of the hotel and resort Uncle Clark was building.

A large sign said, "Perry Construction: The Future Home of the Pine Creek Pass Resort."

Uncle Clark touched a button on his dashboard and the gate on the fence slid to one side. They drove through.

A man in a security uniform stepped out of a small hut nearby. He waved at them.

They followed the road to the main construction area. There was a large building straight ahead. Two other buildings spread out left and right from it like wings.

Nick said, "Wow! You've done a lot of work since I was here last summer."

"We're behind schedule," Uncle Clark said. "We had to change a few things because of the archaeological find."

Nick remembered that the workers had found some really old artifacts while they were digging a few months ago. The area had been sealed off to protect whatever they'd found.

"Let's have a look," Uncle Clark said. He drove around to the left. They came to an area that had been fenced off from everything else. In the middle of the fence was a large shed-type building. It looked like a warehouse.

"Where is everybody?" Andrew asked as they climbed out of the truck.

"We don't work on Sundays," Uncle Clark said. He went to a small door in the fence. He took out a key and unlocked it. Then they walked to the door of the big shed. Uncle Clark unlocked that door.

The four of them walked in. Uncle Clark grabbed a huge handle on a panel and switched on some lights.

Nick was surprised. The entire shed

was like its own construction zone. Wooden planks zigzagged through large ditches and holes.

"The archaeologists from Denver keep finding more stuff," Uncle Clark said.

"What kind of stuff?" asked Andrew.

Mr. Perry stepped to the edge of one of the ditches. "They think they found the site of a Franciscan mission built in the early-1700s."

"I thought they didn't have missions here until the 1800s," Andrew said.

"That's what we thought—until we found this," Uncle Clark said.

Nick peered into one of the holes. It was deeper than he thought. Inside he saw what looked like stone walls and part of a door.

Uncle Clark said, "All we can find is a reference to someone named Father Juan. We can't find a record of him anywhere else. It's a mystery. But our experts think this mission might be the earliest in Colorado."

"Even before Zebulon Pike found Pikes Peak?" Andrew asked.

Nick wasn't a history buff like his brother. But he knew enough to be impressed.

"Let me show you something," Uncle Clark said. He led them to a wall with large tables. He went to one in the middle.

On the table was something that looked like a toy shack made out of twigs and pieces of wood.

"What is it?" Mr. Perry asked.

"A stable," Uncle Clark said. He pulled a white cover off of the next table.

Nick did a double-take at what he saw. On the table were carved figures of Mary and Joseph and a baby Jesus. Next to them were other figures of what might have been shepherds and the Wise Men.

Nick's dad leaned in close. "Are these from the dig?" he asked.

"Yes," Uncle Clark said.

"These were carved by the mission-
aries?" Andrew asked.

Uncle Clark nodded. "You can pick
them up," he said.

"Be careful," Nick's dad said.

Nick picked up the figure of Joseph.
He was astonished by the detail in such
an old carving. He could see the lines of
the robe and even the shape of the beard.

"We think they were painted at one
time," Uncle Clark said.

Mr. Perry held up the figure of Mary.

"Everyone should see this," he said.

Uncle Clark nodded. "I've talked to Father Cliff. I'm going to lend this to St. Clare's to put on display for Christmas."

"Amazing!" Andrew said.

***

They returned to the truck. Uncle Clark stopped before he got in and gave a loud, sharp whistle.

Nick wasn't sure why. He looked around. Then, from around one of the half-done buildings, a dog came running. The dog had short brown hair, a long nose, and big pointy ears that stuck straight up.

"Is that Jake?" Nick's dad asked.

"It sure is," Uncle Clark said.

Jake bounded toward his owner, barking happily. Uncle Clark bent down to give him a hug. He scratched behind the dog's ears.

"You leave him up here?" Mr. Perry asked.

"The construction crew loves him. And he's good at security," Uncle Clark said. "He has his own little house down by the security hut."

"I didn't know you had a dog," Nick said.

Uncle Clark rubbed Jake's face and said, "He gets a bit wild when I take him into town. He likes to jump on people and overdo it with the licking. So, I keep him away."

Andrew asked, "Is he going with us?"

Uncle Clark whistled again. Jake jumped into the cab of the pickup truck. He scrambled over the front seat and joined the two boys in the back. He sniffed and licked at Andrew and Nick.

Nick petted Jake's back. "Hey, Jake!" he said.

"Calm down!" Andrew said, pushing at Jake to sit down.

"See what I mean?" Uncle Clark said.

They drove up a back road around the construction site. They came to another gate. This time he had to get out and unlock it. Nick's dad leapt out and relocked it once they drove through. They followed the road further up into the mountain.

"Do you own all this land?" Nick asked.

"The Perry family owns it," his dad answered. "Our family has been buying more and more over the past few decades."

"This is a good spot. There are smaller trees in that direction," Uncle Clark said. He brought the truck to a halt.

They climbed out of the truck.

Uncle Clark reached behind the back seat and pulled out a rifle. Then he reached in and brought out another one. He handed it to his brother.

Nick and Andrew looked at each other.

"We're going to *shoot* down the Christmas tree?" Nick said.

The men laughed.

"There are mountain lions and bears for us to think about," Uncle Clark said. "We've had a few show up at the construction site."

"You boys climb in the back of the truck and get the axes and saws."

"No chain saw?" Nick said.

"Not allowed in Colorado," Uncle Clark said.

Nick frowned. He and Andrew got the tools from a metal chest in the truck bed.

Uncle Clark slung the rifle onto his shoulder and took the axe.

They trekked into the forest. Jake ran off in different directions, but always came rushing back to them. They reached a clearing where smaller trees stood.

Uncle Clark said, "There was fire caused by a lightning strike a few years back. That's why some of these trees are smaller. Do you see one you like?"

The other three Perrys looked around. Finally, Nick pointed and said, "I like this one."

Mr. Perry looked the tree over and said, "A Douglas fir. It has a great shape. Nice and full. Not too tall for our ceiling. And it's got good clearance from the other trees." He patted Nick on the back. "Good choice."

They set about the work of cutting down the tree. Each took turns with the axe and handsaw. Uncle Clark kept an eye out for any wildlife. Nick felt like it took a long, long time to cut through the thick bark.

Then: "Timber!" Andrew called out. The tree tipped over onto the ground.

Nick watched as his dad and Andrew positioned themselves at the top and base of the tree. Then they lifted it up. Uncle Clark led the way back to the truck.

"Grab the tools!" Mr. Perry called back to Nick.

Uncle Clark whistled for Jake, but the dog wasn't around.

Nick picked up the axe. He was about to pick up the handsaws when he thought he heard Jake bark from somewhere deeper in the woods. He moved in the direction of the sound.

He knew he was walking in the opposite direction from the pickup truck. He kept looking back to make sure he didn't forget where he was.

"Jake!" he called out.

He heard something rustling off to the right. He paused. He couldn't see anything.

"Jake?" he called again.

He walked in the direction of the rustling sound. Nothing was there. Then he thought he saw movement off to his left. He turned to move that way and then saw something brown-colored

low to the ground.

"Come on, Jake," Nick said.

The brown thing began to move slowly to its right.

It wasn't Jake. It was a mountain lion.

CHAPTER THIRTEEN

Call of the Wild

Nick froze where he was, but his mind raced. He tried to remember what he was taught about what to do if he ever encountered a mountain lion.

Should he run?

The lion kept moving to its right. Nick realized it was trying to circle around him.

Then Nick remembered. If he ever encountered a mountain lion, he shouldn't turn his back on it. Mountain lions like to attack their prey from behind and get them by the neck. *Face the lion and try to look bigger than you are,* Nick thought. *Or was that for a bear?*

Nick didn't care. He held the axe in both hands and lifted it up over his head.

"Go away!" Nick shouted at the lion.

The lion continued to circle around Nick.

As loud as he could, Nick shouted, "DAD!"

His voice echoed all around.

The mountain lion flinched at the shout but kept its eyes on Nick and kept moving around.

The axe was getting heavier in Nick's hands. His arms began to ache. He felt sweat break out on his forehead. What should he do if the mountain lion attacked?

"DAD!" he shouted again. "UNCLE CLARK!"

The mountain lion kept moving slowly to get around Nick. Nick slowly turned to face it.

Then the lion stopped. There was a clear line between Nick and the animal. No trees or branches. The lion crouched.

Nick realized it was going to try for him.

"DAD!" Nick screamed. He tightened his hands around the axe handle. All he could think was to swing it down onto the lion if it came at him. And hope he wouldn't miss.

Nick swallowed hard.

The mountain lion sprang for him.

Nick stumbled back. He fell on his backside.

This is it, he thought and screamed.

Just then Jake leapt in between the lion and Nick. He growled low, the hair on his back up.

The mountain lion skidded on the dirt and used all four legs to push back. Jake jumped toward it. The lion found its footing and scrambled backwards.

Nick struggled to get to his feet.

Jake barked and snarled, moving slowly at the lion.

The animal kept backing up. It looked for a way around the dog.

Nick held the axe like a baseball bat, ready to swing.

Jake kept a steady pace toward the lion.

Then there was a loud *pop* like a firecracker. The bark of a tree next to the mountain lion exploded. The lion jumped—and then scrambled away.

Jake started after the beast, but a loud whistle stopped him in his tracks.

Nick looked through the trees. Uncle Clark and his father were coming closer with their rifles held up and ready. Andrew followed them. He was carrying the handsaws.

At that moment Nick had a silly thought. *Was Andrew going to attack the mountain lion with a handsaw?* It made him want to laugh.

He slumped to the ground and started to cry instead.

***

"You'll suffer a bit of shock," Uncle Clark said when they got to the pickup truck.

His dad was carrying him. "Lie down on the back seat," his dad said. Nick obeyed. His dad climbed in next to him and covered him with his coat.

Andrew sat in the front but kept turning to look at Nick.

"You're a brave boy," his dad said softly as he stroked Nick's hair.

"You did all the right things," Uncle Clark said.

"Who shot at it?" Nick had asked through clenched teeth. He didn't know why he was clenching his teeth together. He didn't feel cold. But he was shaking, too.

"I did," said Uncle Clark. "I didn't want to hit it. Just scare it away."

"Are you sure you aren't hurt?" his dad asked.

"My butt hurts from when I fell down," Nick said. "I might have a splinter."

Andrew laughed.

"Where's Jake?" Nick said. "He saved my life."

Saying the words made Nick want to cry again.

"He's in the back," Uncle Clark said. "He's too riled up to ride in the cab."

"I should get him something for Christmas," Nick said. Or maybe he thought it. He wasn't sure.

Nick heard whispering. He looked up. His father's eyes were closed. He was praying.

They arrived home. Nick's mom and two sisters were fluttering around him. It made Nick think of birds. Lizzy was smiling at him as if she knew something he didn't know. Sam kept watching him and looked like she'd been crying again. *It's too much fuss*, he wanted to tell everyone. *I'm all right.*

Nick's mom insisted that he have a hot bath.

"I don't need a bath," Nick said.

"I want you to relax, be calm," she said.

"I'm calm," he said. But he wasn't. He kept imagining the moment when the mountain lion came at him.

"You have a bath while we set up the tree," his dad said.

"I want to hang ornaments," Nick said.

"We'll decorate the tree later," his mom said.

She drew the bath for him and left while he undressed. He sunk into the hot water. It felt good. He closed his eyes. He could hear the murmuring of voices from downstairs. He heard the front door slam and the pickup truck start up outside.

I didn't get to say goodbye to Jake, Nick thought.

He lay in the water. The faucet dripped. He breathed in and out and could hear the sound of it. He thought about what a strange Advent it was.

This stuff never happened in Denver, he thought.

He heard the sound of Christmas music playing downstairs. He couldn't make out the song.

Wait 'til Brad hears about this, he thought.

CHAPTER FOURTEEN

The Faded Flower

Sam always heard that twins experienced weird things.

While Nick was away to get the Christmas tree, Sam felt anxious. She thought it was because she'd made such a mess with the pizza. But she knew it was more than that. She felt a kind of fear and she didn't know why.

When the phone call came about what had happened with the mountain lion, Sam sneaked away to her room and cried.

Lizzy came in to see her. "Why are you crying?" she asked.

Sam shook her head. "Was Nick's guardian angel there?"

"Our guardian angels never leave us," she said.

"But what if something happened? What if Nick—?" She didn't finish her question.

Lizzy gazed at her. "Do you think God still loves us even when really bad things happen?"

Sam didn't know how to answer.

Lizzy looked over at something on Sam's desk. Sam followed her eyes. She was looking at a small nativity set that Sam put out every Christmas.

Lizzy gave a deep sigh. "Jesus was born so he could die for us. We celebrate Christmas so we can celebrate Easter."

Where does she get these thoughts? Sam wondered.

Sam wasn't surprised that Nick was the center of attention the next day. Some of the kids kept saying the mountain lion story didn't really happen. Others had heard that Nick killed the mountain lion with an axe.

Brad started calling Nick "The Lion King."

Lance walked up to Sam and said, "Your brother is my hero" and walked away again.

In the afternoon Nick walked into the Christmas pageant rehearsal and the choir began to sing "The Lion Sleeps Tonight."

"Very funny," Nick said.

Sam thought Nick was unusually quiet throughout the day. Until Mrs. Hecht had to yell at him for jumping on the small trampoline again.

"But I was flying!" Nick said.

Sam was having a hard time memorizing her lines for Mary. Kim said them perfectly. Sam thought that maybe Kim had learned them so well just to show who should have gotten the part.

Or maybe it was because Kim was really smart.

Sam started to feel nervous. The big program wasn't far away. Why did she think she could get up in front of everyone and play Mary?

She asked Mary for help.

She thought she heard a voice say, "Do your best."

She looked around. No one was speaking to her.

Do your best.

Okay. She would.

During the ride home from school that afternoon, Mrs. Perry reminded the kids that they were going to sing carols at the retirement center that night.

Sam had remembered. Andrew groaned.

Lizzy said, "I wonder if they'll have

Christmas cookies."

Sam had no idea why she said that.

"I just suffered a bad experience, so I shouldn't go," Nick said. He was faking it.

Mrs. Perry knew it. "You're going. You can tell them all about what happened. They probably have stories of their own."

"Like when they shot a mountain lion with one of their muskets," Andrew said.

The kids laughed.

"They're not *that* old," their mother said.

Nick gave Sam a look that said *oh yes they are*.

The Perry family joined other families from Saint Clare's at the front of the Faded Flower Retirement Home. It was two buildings. One looked like an old mansion. The other was a new building that looked to Sam like a hospital that was trying not to look like a hospital.

They went inside to the area used as a dining room. They found a corner near a piano. Mr. Thompson from the church sat down and began to play Christmas songs. The residents of the home slowly made their way in. Some walked. Some used walkers. Some had electric wheelchairs. Others were in wheelchairs that had to be pushed.

"Let's go," Mr. Thompson said to the makeshift choir.

They gathered in close and held pages with the words to the songs.

They started with "Hark! The Herald Angels Sing."

Some of the residents sang along.

Sam stood between Lizzy and Nick. Nick kept changing some of the words to sillier ones. Sam had to fight to keep from getting the giggles.

They sang a few songs and then spread out to help serve the dinner.

"It's so lovely to have you here," one woman said to Sam.

An old man who smelled like pepper-

mint shook Sam's hand. "You are a darling girl," he said. He fished in the pocket of his sweater and pulled out a piece of candy. "This is for you."

Sam looked at the candy. It was something brown and had bits of fuzz all over it. She thanked him and waited until he looked away to wrap the candy in a napkin and throw it away.

"When I was your age...," Sam heard someone say to Lizzy.

She glanced over at Andrew. He was talking to a man wearing a baseball cap with some kind of military symbol on it.

Nick was at another table saying, "It was a really *big* mountain lion with really sharp teeth."

Her parents were passing plates of food to various tables. She heard her mother speaking in Spanish to a small man in a wheelchair.

In the middle of dinner, they gathered around the piano and sang a few more

Christmas songs.

Then they went around to serve dessert.

Lizzy came up to Sam. She was carrying a tray with the dinner and a slice of apple pie. "The manager asked us to take this to Mrs. Daniels in Room 102. She's not well."

"Okay," Sam said.

The two girls followed the signs pointing to the hall with Room 102. They found it without trouble. Sam knocked on the open door.

The room was like a little apartment. There were pictures of family on the wall and ornaments and books on the shelves. A small TV sat on a stand near the large window.

Mrs. Daniels was a white-haired woman with pale wrinkled skin. Sam thought the room number must be her age. But she had blue eyes that were bright and shiny.

Sam pulled a tray over to the bed. Lizzy put the tray down in front of Mrs. Daniels.

"Thank you," Mrs. Daniels said. Her voice was light but raspy.

"You're welcome," Lizzy said. She moved to the foot of the bed next to Sam.

Mrs. Daniels took the fork and knife in shaky hands. She began to cut up her food. She looked up at the girls.

"They're impressive," Mrs. Daniels said.

Sam wasn't sure what she meant. Then Sam realized that she wasn't looking at her or Lizzy. She was looking at something behind them.

Sam turned. There was nothing there.

"What is?" Lizzy asked.

"Your friends," she said. She took a bite of her dinner.

"What friends?" Sam asked. She wondered if Mrs. Daniels had something wrong in her head.

Mrs. Daniels gestured with her fork. "Your friends behind you. Your angels."

Sam's mouth dropped open.

Lizzy looked surprised. "You can see them?" she asked.

The old woman smiled. "I think you can, too," she said.

Lizzy nodded. "Sometimes I can."

Mrs. Daniels and Lizzy exchanged a look that made Sam feel left out. "I haven't seen mine," she said sadly.

Mrs. Daniels moved her head up and down. "Maybe you will one day. And maybe you won't. Don't fret about it.

Just be glad he's there."

"Can you tell me what he looks like?" Sam asked.

"Big. Strong. *Large* wings when they're spread out." She chuckled. "His hand is on your shoulder."

Sam looked to her left shoulder and then her right. "Which one?"

"Your left," she said.

Sam reached up and touched her shoulder.

"If only you could see how big his hand is," Mrs. Daniels said. "Your hand is like one of his fingers."

"I call him Raphael," Lizzy said.

Mrs. Daniels was trying to cut a slice of the meat. "That's nice. Does your angel have a name?" she asked Sam.

"I haven't thought of one," Sam said. "And some people say it's not good to ask."

"That may be true," said Mrs. Daniels.

Sam asked, "Can you ask our angels

if they were at the Birth of Jesus?'

"I don't have to," Mrs. Daniels said. "They *all* were."

There was a crash in the hallway. Lizzy and Sam rushed out to investigate. Nick was standing over an upturned tray. Next to him was a man in a wheelchair. A nurse rushed up.

Nick was flustered. "He tried to run me over with his wheelchair!"

The man in the wheelchair chuckled.

"Not *again*," the nurse said and grabbed the handles of the wheelchair. "Back to your room, Mr. Peleg. These people are only trying to help."

The man in the wheelchair kept his eyes on Nick. "Good thing you're a fast mover!" he said. He chuckled again.

"Don't be so grouchy," the nurse said to Mr. Peleg as they disappeared into a room.

The piano started to play in the dining room again.

"We have to go back," Lizzy said.

The two girls went back in to Mrs. Daniels' room, but she wasn't in her bed. They saw that the bathroom door was closed.

"Goodnight!" Lizzy called out.

"Goodnight! Thank you!" came a voice from the other side of the door.

Sam was glad that they came to the retirement home.

CHAPTER FIFTEEN

Surprises

"These are our last few days of rehearsals, so I want everyone to *concentrate*," Mrs. Hecht said to the cast.

The stage was now decorated the way it was supposed to look for their performance. The angels were on a tall platform on the left side. The choir was on the right. In the center was the stable. It looked like a combination of a wooden shed that had been attached to a cave. There were green shapes that were supposed to look like palm trees.

Plastic plants in pots were scattered all over the place.

Nick sat and watched as the shepherds kept bumping into the Roman guards as they went on and off stage. The villagers of Bethlehem were played by the first and second graders. They kept wandering in *front* of Mary and Joseph and the crib.

"Not *this* way, *that* way!" Mrs. Hecht said over and over. Then she shouted, "Where are my angels?"

Nick ran onto the stage and climbed the stairs behind the platform. He and Brad and the other angels bumped into each other as they took their places.

"Be careful up there!" Mrs. Hecht said.

Nick looked up. Wires were dangling from the ceiling, but no cardboard angels were attached.

"I guess they won't have flying angels after all," Nick said.

Brad smiled. "They still could," he said.

"What do you mean?" asked Nick.

Brad pointed at the side of the platform. The small trampoline was there.

"Oh—I didn't see that," Nick said.

"Because I put plants around it," Brad said.

Nick looked at Brad. "Why did you hide it there?"

"If you jump on it from up here, then you'll *really* fly," he said.

"If *I* jump? Why would I jump?" Nick asked.

"Because that's all you've been talking about!" Brad said.

Nick looked down at the trampoline, then over at Brad. "*You* jump," he said.

Brad frowned. "And break my neck? No way."

"What are you guys talking about?" asked Ellis Kent. He was an angel on the other side of Brad.

"Flying," Brad said.

"I'd love to fly," Ellis said. "Show me how."

Mrs. Hecht shouted at them. "Angels! Pay attention! It's your line!"

The shepherds were looking up at them.

Nick and the other angels said, "Glory to God in the highest and on earth *peace* to people of good will!"

"You need to say it *together*," Mrs. Hecht said.

She made them say it again. And again. And again.

"Sit down and wait where you are," Mrs. Hecht told them.

Nick sat down on the edge of the platform. Ellis Kent was whispering to Brad. Brad then turned to Nick.

"Guess what?"

"What?" Nick asked.

"The animals are here," said Brad.

"What animals?" asked Nick.

"The ones from the petting zoo," Brad said. "They put them in a pen behind the school."

"Even a camel?" Nick asked.

"Maybe even an elephant," Brad said.

Nick heard a loud sneeze. He looked at his sister. She was dressed as Mary and standing in the middle of the stage with Lance. She was looking unhappy. Lance was wiping his nose on the sleeve of his peasant outfit.

"Lance!" Mrs. Hecht called out. "Use a tissue!"

"Sorry!" he said.

"Are you catching a cold?" Mrs. Hecht asked him.

"No, ma'am!" he said quickly.

"Good thing he wasn't wearing his beard," Nick said loudly.

Sam frowned at him.

"Lines!" Mrs. Hecht shouted.

"Joseph!" Sam said. "My time has come!"

Lance took her hand. Sam jerked it back. "I will find a place for you to give birth!" he said.

A girl from the fifth grade stepped onto the stage. Nick knew she was the innkeeper's wife.

"What do you people want?" the innkeeper's wife said. "Stop crowding my doorway!"

"But Mrs. Innkeeper's Wife," Lance said. "My wife is about to have a baby! Please give us a place to stay!"

"Oh!" Sam cried out and held the pillow tucked in her dress.

"I have no room!" the innkeeper's wife said.

"Anywhere!" Lance countered. "A closet or a garage or a small box!"

The innkeeper's wife put a finger to her chin. "Come to think of it. I have a stable. You can stay there."

"Thank you! Thank you!" Lance said, jumping up and down. He turned to Sam. "Mary, we have a place to stay!"

And then he did something that Nick thought he would never ever see on a stage at Saint Clare's Catholic School.

Lance grabbed Sam by the shoulders and kissed her on the lips.

Everyone on stage gasped.

Nick's eyes went wide as saucers.

Brad snorted.

And then Nick saw something he thought he would never see anywhere in the world. He saw Mary punch Joseph in the jaw.

It wasn't a hard punch. More like a light slap with knuckles. But Lance stumbled back into the crib and fell over onto a big beanbag pillow that was decorated to look like a sheep.

"Lance!" Sam cried out. She began to spit and sputter and wipe at her mouth.

"That's it!" Mrs. Hecht shouted. "Lance! Come see me this instant!"

Nick watched Sam rush off the stage. He thought about jumping down from the platform to follow her, but Kim was already hot on her heels.

Lance crawled off the beanbag sheep and slunk off the stage to Mrs. Hecht. "I'm calling your parents," she said to him.

Nick turned to Brad. At the same time, the two boys burst into unrestrained laugher.

***

Nick was far more impressed by the animals from the petting zoo than he expected to be.

Mr. Norm stood next to the pen he'd constructed. It was really the nursery school playground. It already had a fence around it. But now there were fences inside the big fence to separate some of the animals.

Mr. Norm was leaning on one of the posts. He adjusted the toothpick he always had in his mouth. Kids from the school had gathered to look.

Nick and Brad drew closer to the fence. There were two sheep by the sliding board. A goat was trying to chew on the leather swing seat. Ducks and chickens wandered under the monkey bars. A llama stood by the other end of the fence looking very tall and bored. A buffalo was in a pen of its own. It was eating feed.

"The buffalo is named Cody," Mr. Norm said. "After Wyoming. Because that's where he came from."

A donkey stood in the far corner of the pen. He gazed at them.

"That's Chaser," Mr. Norm said.

"Why's he called 'Chaser'?" Nick asked.

Mr. Norm tilted his head and eyed the animal. "Because we always seem to be chasing him," he said. "He escapes every chance he gets. I don't know where he thinks he's going, but he goes."

"Can we pet them?" one of the kids asked.

"Not today," Mr. Norm said. "They're still agitated from the ride over. I wouldn't want anyone to get hurt."

"No camels?" Nick said.

Mr. Norm laughed. "Camels? Who said anything about camels?"

"I heard a rumor," Nick said.

"Wouldn't it be fun to have a camel?" Mr. Norm said. He seemed to like the idea.

Nick thought about it. "Are they going to put some of the animals on the stage?"

Mr. Norm said, "That would get messy."

"Then why are they here?" Brad asked.

Mr. Norm gave a slight shrug. "The idea is to show people what kinds of animals were in the stable."

"Did they have *buffalos* in Bethlehem?" Nick asked.

Mr. Norm gave him a smile. "Do you know that they didn't?"

Nick didn't.

There was a chirping sound. The boys wondered where it came from until Mr. Norm took a cell phone out of one of his overall pockets.

"Hello," he said to someone. He looked surprised. "Oh! All right. I'll be right there." He hung up. "I have to find a place for a cow. Nobody said they were bringing a cow."

He started to walk off, but then turned around again. "Stay away from the animals! Don't touch and"—he looked at Nick and Brad—"*keep out!*"

Mr. Norm strode off.

Brad turned to the other kids. "You heard what he said. Go away. It's time to leave the animals to rest."

The kids looked puzzled.

"Go on," Brad said and shooed them away. "We should guard them to make sure they're all right," he said to Nick.

"Really?" Nick asked. "My mom is probably waiting to take me home."

"Don't you want a picture first?" Brad took out his phone. "Let's get a picture."

Brad tried to position himself so the animals were in the background. The animals moved.

"I wish we could get on one," Brad said.

Nick looked at the llama, then the buffalo. "Not a chance," he said.

"What about the donkey? He's just standing there," Brad said.

The two boys walked around to the donkey's side of the pen. Brad tried to position himself in a picture with

Chaser. Chaser turned around so his backside was facing the camera.

"He did that on purpose!" Nick said with a laugh.

Brad started to climb the fence.

"What are you doing?" Nick asked.

"I'm getting a picture on that donkey," Brad said. "Come on."

Nick looked around. "But what if we get caught?"

"No one is watching," Brad said. He was already on top of the fence.

The donkey seemed to know what Brad wanted. It moved alongside the fence.

"See? He wants me to get on," Brad said. He tossed the phone to Nick. "Take a picture of me."

"My grandfather had a donkey he let me ride," Brad said as he climbed from the fence over to the donkey's back. "Good Chaser. Nice Chaser."

Nick grabbed hold of the fence and

pulled himself up. "Smile," he said to Brad. He snapped the picture.

Brad gestured to Nick. "Get on. I'll get a picture of both of us."

"Well..." Nick thought about it. But only for a second. He reached over. Brad grabbed his hand and pulled. Nick was on the donkey's back.

Nick handed the phone to Brad.

"Okay," Brad said.

But Chaser started to move.

"What's he doing?" Nick asked.

"He thinks we want a ride," Brad answered.

"What do we do?" Nick asked.

"We ride," said Brad.

Chaser moved around the playground in a circle. The boys hung on while they bounced up and down.

"I can't get the picture," Brad said, bouncing.

"I want to get off," Nick said.

Chaser was moving at a pace that

made Nick nervous. He was afraid of hurting himself if he jumped.

"How do we get him to stop?" Nick asked.

"Normally you say 'whoa.'"

"Then say it!"

"Whoa," Brad said.

Nick joined in. "Whoa."

Chaser wasn't slowing down. He was speeding up.

The ducks and chickens scattered. The sheep and goat took cover under the sliding board. The llama snorted at them. The buffalo looked uninterested.

"What are you two doing?" Mr. Norm called out to them. "What did I tell you?"

"Make him stop," Nick called back.

Mr. Norm grumbled, then opened the latch on the main fence. He stepped inside the pen and moved for Chaser.

As soon as Chaser saw Mr. Norm, he moved away. Mr. Norm said, "Now stop it, Chaser. I mean it."

Whichever direction Mr. Norm went, Chaser quickly shifted to the other direction. The boys hung on for dear life.

"You're getting him agitated," Mr. Norm said.

"It's not us!" Brad said.

Suddenly Nick realized that Mr. Norm had left the gate open.

"Mr. Norm!" Nick called out. "The gate!"

Mr. Norm saw his mistake. "Oh no," he said and tried to run back.

It was too late. Chaser saw the open gate. He bolted.

Nick didn't know donkeys could move so fast.

"Stop!" Brad cried out.

"Whoa!" Nick shouted.

Chaser headed for the church. Father Cliff stepped out of the door with an armload of books. He saw the donkey and the boys. "Hey!" he shouted. The books fell from his arms. He made a move to intercept the donkey.

Chaser dodged to the right. He headed for the school and the parking lot.

"No!" Nick yelled.

There were cars in line to pick up students. Other cars were moving around the parking lot. Nick saw his family's minivan.

"Oh no," he said. He wanted to cover his face, but didn't dare let go of the donkey.

He saw his mom stare at them as they raced past.

Some of the cars hit their brakes. A few honked their horns. The noise spooked Chaser. He picked up speed.

"Stop, please stop, please stop," Brad was saying.

People were getting out of the cars and rushing from the school. Chaser was earning his name. He got to the end of the parking lot and turned to the open stretch of lawn that bordered the church property. It led to the road.

Nick groaned. There was nothing to stop Chaser from riding into traffic or the town.

A car stopped on the road. A woman leapt out and stood directly ahead of them. Chaser ran straight for her.

The woman shouted in a clear voice, "Chaser! *Halt!*"

Chaser stopped dead in his tracks as if he'd hit a brick wall.

The boys were not prepared for it. They both flew off the front of the donkey.

As he flew through the air, Nick thought two things.

I wish I had on my angel costume
and
I'm in big trouble.

Then he hit the ground hard.

CHAPTER SIXTEEN

Hard

"Eight weeks," Dr. Osbourne said as she finished putting the cast on Nick's left wrist. She was talking to Nick's mother and father. They stood near him in one of the rooms in the Emergency Ward. They both had worried looks.

Nick was hardly listening. He was in too much pain.

"Since there's no head injury, I can prescribe painkillers," Dr. Osbourne said.

Nick wanted painkillers now.

Dr. Osbourne looked at Nick. "Be

glad it's a simple break. Some broken wrists get complicated."

Nick nodded.

"And be glad you weren't trampled by that donkey," she added. "I've had people in here who were pretty bad off. Especially with Chaser."

"You know Chaser?" Mrs. Perry asked.

"*Everyone* knows Chaser," the doctor said. "It's a good thing he listens to Maggie."

"Maggie" was Maggie Sullivan, Mr. Norm's sister. She owned all of the animals they had brought to the school.

"Otherwise, you might be halfway to Denver now," Dr. Osbourne said. She stood up. "I'll give you a brochure about the cast. Don't get it wet and all that. We'll follow up in a few days."

Nick's parents thanked her. She pulled the curtain aside and stepped out.

"Well?" Mr. Perry said to his son.

"How is Brad?" Nick asked.

Mrs. Perry said, "He's in another room. Seven stitches in his head. They have to watch for a concussion."

"I can explain everything," Nick said.

"Sensibly? Intelligently?" Mr. Perry asked.

Nick lowered his head. "No."

"I didn't think so," he said. "Let's go home."

***

Various people had filmed Nick and Brad riding on Chaser. There they were racing across the parking lot with terror on their faces. Another showed Maggie Sullivan shouting for Chaser to stop and then Nick and Brad flying like rag dolls over the top and onto the ground.

It was on the social networks by the evening. A Denver news channel showed it on the Nine O'Clock news. They had an interview with Father Cliff

explaining why the animals were there. And Mr. Norm tugged at the toothpick in his mouth in another interview and said, "I warned those boys to stay off." The television reporter finished up by saying that the two boys were treated for minor injuries.

"Minor?" Nick said. He looked down at his cast. Then he looked over at his parents.

"Mountain lions and broken wrists," his mother said. "This was not a good week for you to play an angel."

Nick frowned. He wouldn't be playing

an angel at all now. Brad was taken out of the pageant, too.

His father turned off the television. "The irony is that this will be great publicity for the Nativity program."

Sam walked into the family room and dropped down onto the couch next to her parents.

"Are you all right?" her mother asked. "You look flushed."

Sam shook her head.

Her mother put a hand to her forehead. "I think you have a fever."

Sam leaned onto her mother's shoulder and closed her eyes.

Nick looked at his parents. They gave each other their *uh oh* look.

Chapter Seventeen

Bad News

Sam lay in bed. Her fever had broken in the middle of the night. She slowly sat up. She felt weak.

This is all your fault, Lance.

Somewhere in another part of the house an alarm went off. The house was to get moving for the day. This was the last morning of school before the Christmas break. That afternoon was the Saint Clare's Catholic School Christmas pageant.

She hoped she was well enough to

play Mary. She had been waiting such a long time.

A gust of wind bumped the window. Maybe it was finally snowing?

Sam got up. She swayed a little. Then she went to window and pushed the curtain aside. It was dark. The lawns and street looked as they always did. No snow.

She heard footsteps in the hall. A light came on and a yellow line shone through her door. The knob turned and the door opened. Her mother peeked in. She looked at the bed, then squinted and saw Sam by the window.

"Hi," she said softly and came in. She turned on the overhead light. Sam squinted. "How are you feeling?" she asked.

Sam said, "A little better." But the words didn't come out in the sound of her voice. It was more like a harsh croak, like someone had replaced her voice with a birthday party noisemaker.

Sam tried to clear her throat.

"A little—" but the sound was the same.

"Try whispering," her mother said.

"I feel a little better," Sam whispered. "But what's wrong with my voice?"

"Does your throat hurt?" her mother asked.

Sam swallowed. It hurt a little. "Kinda," Sam whispered.

Mrs. Perry put a hand to her daughter's forehead. "No fever."

"My voice," Sam whispered again. She was worried.

"Laryngitis," her mother said. "Your vocal chords are swollen."

Sam's eyes grew wide. She whispered, "Will I be able to talk by this afternoon?"

Her mother pulled her close for a hug. Her mom's robe was soft. It smelled of flowers. "I'm sorry, Sam," she said.

Her mom was able to get Sam in to see their doctor later that morning. Dr. Forrest gave them a prescription to help any pain in her throat. But he made it clear that she needed to rest her voice. She couldn't be in the Christmas pageant.

Sam felt too tired to cry. The disappointment simply worked through her like a dull ache.

Kim will be happy, she thought.

"May I take her to the pageant?" Mrs. Perry asked the doctor.

"She doesn't have a fever," he said. "I don't think she's contagious. She can go if she feels well enough." He looked at Sam. "Just don't hug or kiss anyone," he said.

Lance, Sam thought. She was going to have to work on forgiving Lance.

***

Nick sat in class. Sister Lucy had them doing a "musical math assignment," as she called it. They were singing "The

Twelve Days of Christmas" and adding up all the presents in the song. They were up to thirty-six.

Nick wondered what the "me" in the song did with all that stuff.

His wrist itched underneath his cast.

Mrs. Hecht came to the door and peered in. She signaled for Sister Lucy to send out Kim and Billy Boyd.

The new Mary and Joseph, Nick thought.

He looked over at Sam's empty desk. He knew she was sad about getting sick.

He glanced over at Brad. Brad was wearing a baseball cap. Normally hats weren't allowed to be worn inside the school. But Brad needed one to cover his stitches—and hide his shaved head.

Nick and Brad were no longer playing angels in the pageant.

That was bad enough, but the worst part was that Brad had dropped his phone during their wild ride on Chaser.

The phone got trampled, along with the photos he'd taken.

Mr. Norm offered for them to sit on Chaser and take another picture.

The boys declined. They never wanted to ride a donkey again.

***

Sam rested on the couch in the family room. For a while she looked at the lights on the Christmas tree. They blinked red and green and white and blue.

It was their family tradition to put the lights on when they got the tree. Then they put the rest of the decorations on the tree on Christmas Eve.

She read a book about a boy and a girl who travel back in time to the Birth of Jesus.

She wondered what that would be like. *No Christmas trees there*, she thought. *No snow.*

In the book, the boy and girl met one of the angels who had appeared to the shepherds. His name was Hosea. He helped a lame shepherd boy go to the stable to see Jesus. The shepherd boy led the boy and girl to the manger.

Her eyes went to Lizzy's "Jesse Tree" hanging on the wall. Raphael was watching her.

"I'm going to call my angel Hosea," she whispered. "I hope he'll help me feel well enough to go to the Christmas pageant."

Sam's mom came in with a bowl of soup. "Chicken noodle," she said.

After Sam ate the soup, she got up and helped her mom put up a few decorations around the house. It felt a little like a holiday.

Her mom made her lie down again until it was time to go to the Christmas pageant.

***

Sam sat with her mom and dad in the main hall at the school. Every seat was taken. People stood along the back wall. Almost everyone had their phones held up and ready to take pictures.

Sam looked around. She saw Nick sitting in another row with Brad. He wiggled his fingers at her. She wiggled her fingers back.

The curtains opened on the stage. The set looked bright and colorful.

The first and second grade choirs were already on the platform. They began to sing a series of Christmas songs that led up to the story of the angel appearing to Mary.

Kim came on as Mary. Then one of the seventh graders entered in one of Lizzy's angel costumes. Sam thought he looked like an angel. They said their lines perfectly.

The choir changed to Sam's class and the fourth graders. They sang while the scene changed to a scene with Mary and her cousin Elizabeth. The choir sang a version of the Magnificat.

Then came the scene when the angels appeared to the shepherds.

Nick and Brad watched the program. Nick thought it was going really well. The shepherds had to be herded onto the stage by Sister Lucy, who was dressed like a shepherd herself.

The choir sang, "While Shepherds

Watched Their Flocks by Night" and "It Came upon a Midnight Clear."

Then the shepherds had to say their lines.

David Coogan stammered, "Behold a great—great—life—*shoot!*—"

"*Light,*" Sister Lucy reminded him.

"*Light!*" he said.

David's family applauded from the back of the room. He turned and bowed to them.

The lights came up on the angels.

"Look at Ellis," Brad whispered. "He's really into it."

Ellis Kent now stood where Nick should have been standing. His face was bright and animated. When they got to the "Glory to God in the highest" lines, he beamed. He really beamed. He spoke as if he really meant it.

"What's he so happy about?" Brad whispered.

Nick had a thought. *Maybe saying*

the words makes him happy. Maybe he believes them. Maybe he really thinks he's an angel appearing to those shepherds.

Nick suddenly realized, *I was so busy thinking about how I looked and being able to fly that I didn't think about what I was doing. The shepherds, the angels, Mary and Joseph . . . we weren't just playacting a story. We're showing something that really happened.*

The choir was made up of the older kids now. They picked up the words and sang, "Glory to God in the highest and on earth, peace to people of good will." Then they sang "Glory to God" in a "round" like "Row, Row, Row Your Boat."

It gave Nick goose bumps, even under his cast.

When the song finished the audience leapt to their feet and clapped.

***

The choir sang "Angels from the Realms of Glory" and then "O Little Town of Bethlehem." Sam didn't expect to be so caught up in the pageant. It became easy for her to forget the fake plants and the hand-painted cardboard and wood. The costumes didn't matter. Sam suddenly felt like their voices were joining with the voices of every kid who ever did a pageant since Jesus was born. They were playing out that first drama again and again.

Then came the scene about the Birth of Jesus.

The lights came up on the stable. Everything looked the way Sam had practiced it. Then one of the sheep actually moved. A duck waddled across the stage. A goat stood nearby blinking at the lights. *The animals are real,* Sam thought. They brought them in after all.

Maggie Sullivan walked on stage dressed as a peasant. She was holding a rope. Then Chaser appeared with Kim as Mary sitting on his back.

Billy Burke, another boy in her class, had replaced Lance as Joseph.

The two of them said their lines as Mary and Joseph. They begged the innkeeper for a place to stay. The innkeeper's wife led them to the stable.

They're great, Sam thought. *Kim is better at being Mary than I would have been.*

She didn't feel sorry for herself. She simply knew it was true. *Kim really was the better choice.* She thought about how she'd waited so long to play the part. Now she wondered if all of her waiting had been for the wrong thing.

Maybe Advent teaches us to learn how to wait for the right thing, she thought.

Maggie Sullivan started to lead Chaser to the side of the stage. Chaser stopped. It was as if he liked being the center of attention. He stood looking at the audience. The audience applauded.

Then Maggie said in a sharp voice, "Chaser. *Move.*"

Chaser knew that command and began to follow her again.

Kim and Billy—as Mary and Joseph—sat in the middle of the stable. Mrs. Rodriguez brought her newborn baby William and put him in Kim's arms. She stepped away and, for a moment, Sam was looking at the very first Nativity scene. Jesus, Mary, and Joseph, together in a place made for animals.

A combined choir sang "Silent Night." Mrs. Hecht asked the audience to sing along. They also sang "The First Noel" and "O Come All Ye Faithful."

Then everything came to a big finish with everyone singing "Joy to the World!"

Sam thought everyone was singing with all their might. She was happy to listen.

The audience gave the kids a long standing ovation.

Nick was on his feet but couldn't applaud. He watched as everyone on stage took bows. Then someone pointed to Mrs. Hecht. She turned to the audience and bowed.

Even Chaser lifted his head up and down like he was bowing to the applause.

Nick glanced up at Ellis. He was looking down at something on the side of the angels' platform.

Nick felt a twinge of panic. "Did you move the trampoline?" Nick whispered to Brad.

"I forgot all about it. Why?" Brad whispered back.

It was too late. Nick watched as Ellis stepped off of the side of the platform. He disappeared behind the row of fake palm trees and then bounced upwards again. Down he went. And then up. Down and up, higher and higher. He was smiling. His arms were spread in a way that said *Look at me! I'm flying!*

The audience began to laugh.

Mrs. Hecht turned to see what had caught their attention.

Sister Lucy made a dash across the stage to stop him.

But Ellis was flying. Even his wings seemed to spread out for it.

That's what I wanted to do, Nick thought.

Then he began to wave his arms. When he dropped and came up again, he had lost his balance. He went down one last time and when he came up, he shot forward into the fake palm trees.

They tipped over and crashed onto the stage. The sheep leapt up and scattered. The goat began to kick with panic. Maggie Sullivan moved to calm the goat. Chaser saw his chance and bolted backstage.

There were bangs and crashes somewhere behind the cast.

Nick saw Ellis lying on the stage.

He slowly sat up. He was rubbing his head. Sister Lucy was at his side now.

Mrs. Hecht was waving for someone to close the curtains. The curtains lurched, then slowly slid closed on the scene.

A few people in the audience clapped again.

"Now *that* was a big finish," Brad said.

Nick shook his head. He knew what would happen next. Mrs. Hecht would want to know, *What was a trampoline doing on the stage?*

And she would figure out who had put it there.

"Get ready for detention," Nick said to Brad. *"A lot* of detention."

CHAPTER EIGHTEEN

Christmas Eve

The days leading up to Christmas were filled with time at home, decorating, Mass, and shopping.

On Christmas Eve, Sam felt the best she had felt in days. Her voice came back. Nick teased her that it was better when she couldn't talk.

The family gathered around the Christmas tree and put on the ornaments.

Mrs. Perry was sad, though. They still hadn't found the missing figurine of Jesus for the crib. Mr. Perry said he would buy one somewhere, but Mrs. Perry wanted one that looked like the original.

They ate a lamb dinner and then opened the last window on the Advent calendar. The question was actually an order: *Share your favorite memory from this Advent.*

Each member of the family took turns. They talked about their first Advent in Hope Springs. Mr. Perry mentioned the decorations downtown and Hagan's Hand-Picked Bookstore. Mrs. Perry loved decorating their new house. Andrew liked how Christmassy it felt in the Virtue Curiosity Shoppe. Lizzy enjoyed creating her angelic "Jesse Tree" and visiting the retirement home. Nick talked about cutting down the Christmas tree and the mountain lion, but Sam noticed he didn't say anything about riding Chaser or his broken arm. Sam said how happy she was to see Kim play Mary in the pageant.

Mr. Perry led them in a prayer of

thanksgiving for their lives and blessings and for the Birth of Jesus.

The time to leave for Midnight Mass came. Everyone dressed up in their best clothes. Even Nick wore a tie.

Saint Clare's was lit almost entirely by candles. The stained glass windows reflected scenes from the Gospels and the figures looked like they were moving in the flickering light.

People had to squeeze into the pews. Chairs were set up in the back and in areas where latecomers could hear.

The grown-up choir sang all the familiar hymns. A quartet played up in the choir loft.

Sam thought it was everything a Midnight Mass was supposed to be.

***

They got home around 1:30 in the morning. The family wandered into the family room. They had a tradition to open just one present before going to bed.

Mr. Perry decided to make hot apple cider for everyone. Sam and Lizzy sat on the couch. Nick and Andrew went to the Christmas tree to decide what presents they wanted to open.

Mrs. Perry drifted over to the nativity set.

She gasped. "How did this get here?" she asked. She turned to the family. "Okay—which one of you did this?"

The family went over to the nativity set. The lost figurine of the baby Jesus was resting in the crib.

"Come on," Mr. Perry said. "Who found him?"

The kids looked at each other. Each one said, "I didn't."

"Lizzy," Mrs. Perry said. "This is the kind of thing you'd do."

Lizzy put up her arms. "I didn't. I promise."

"Then where did it come from?" Mr. Perry asked.

"And who put it in the manger?" Mrs. Perry added.

The family looked at the baby in silence.

"Well," said Mr. Perry. "Merry Christmas, everyone."

"Merry Christmas," they all said.

Nick pointed to the window. "Hey, look. It's snowing!"

Sam sat on the window seat and watched the big fat flakes fall.

She thought, *Maybe this is the best Advent ever.*

Read *MORE* Adventures of Nick & Sam!

Learn more at
AugustineInstitute.org/books

AUGUSTINE INSTITUTE
UNDERSTAND, LIVE, AND SHARE YOUR FAITH